S0-AGE-969

MYSTERY   c.1   91-1100
FER   Ferrars, E. X.
          Smoke without fire

HUNTINGTON CITY-TOWNSHIP
PUBLIC LIBRARY
200 West Market Street
Huntington, IN 46750

SMOKE WITHOUT FIRE

By E. X. Ferrars

E · X · FERRARS

Smoke
Without Fire

DOUBLEDAY
New York   London   Toronto   Sydney   Auckland

Copy-1

HUNTINGTON CITY-TOWNSHIP
PUBLIC LIBRARY
200 West Market Street
Huntington, IN 46750

Crime Club   12291   795 6

PUBLISHED BY DOUBLEDAY
a division of Bantam Doubleday Dell Publishing Group, Inc.
666 Fifth Avenue, New York, New York 10103

DOUBLEDAY and the portrayal of an anchor
with a dolphin are trademarks of Doubleday,
a division of Bantam Doubleday Dell
Publishing Group, Inc.

All the characters in this book are fictitious,
and any resemblance to actual persons, living or
dead, is purely coincidental.

Library of Congress Cataloging-in-Publication Data

Ferrars, E. X.
   Smoke without fire / E. X. Ferrars. — 1st ed. in the United
States of America.
   p. cm.
I. Title.
PR6003.R458S6   1989
823'.912—dc20   90-3544
CIP

ISBN 0-385-26514-x
Copyright © 1989 by M. D. Brown
All Rights Reserved
Printed in the United States of America
January 1991
First Edition in the United States of America

10 9 8 7 6 5 4 3 2 1

SMOKE WITHOUT FIRE

ONE

WHEN THE DOORBELL RANG Andrew Basnett thought that probably he ought to answer it. He was alone in the house, his hosts, Colin and Dorothea Cahill, having set out that morning to the nearby town of Rockford to do some last-minute Christmas shopping. But whoever was ringing no doubt thought that they were at home. He could explain that they would be home soon. He went to the door.

He was a tall man in his mid-seventies. If he had held himself erect as he had when he was younger he would have looked still taller than he did now. He had short but thick grey hair and grey, kindly eyes. He was wearing grey trousers, a brightly patterned cardigan over a green shirt, and grey socks. As often happened, he had forgotten to put on his slippers. He had just finished washing up the breakfast things for the Cahills when the doorbell rang.

The Cahills were old friends. In the days when Andrew had been professor of botany at one of London University's many colleges, Colin had been a very junior member of the staff. He had reached the status of senior lecturer before leaving his post, and taken to relying on the scientific journalism, the occasional TV appearance, and now and then a paperback on the present-day threats to the environment. All this had earned him a modest fame and enough for himself and his wife to live on fairly comfortably, in a very pleasant house near the village of Upper Cullonden, in Berkshire. As if Colin felt that he owed Andrew something for having set his feet on the path to prosperity, he had always kept in touch with him.

At first Andrew had regretted Colin's having abandoned pure science for its merely popular form, but at the same time he had admitted to himself that the young man had really very little originality, while possessing a certain literary gift. Andrew had been touched too by the friendship which had continued even after he had retired and could no longer be of any use to anybody. Yet friends—as he had learnt years ago when his wife Nell had died of cancer and he had been left to learn to endure loneliness—were apt to forget you for most of the year but felt an extraordinary distress at the thought that you might be left to survive Christmas alone. The Cahills were of that order. He generally visited them only once a year, and this was always at Christmas.

He was still drying his hands in the kitchen to go and answer the doorbell when it rang again. He went to the front door and opened it. A man even taller than himself stood there, a very thin man with a long face, a long, thin nose, an almost lipless mouth and small, hard, dark eyes that were not quite level with one another. They gave him an odd look, Andrew thought, of not being quite trustworthy, though why a minor physical defect should have given this impression he would have been at a loss to say. The man was wearing a black beret over grey hair that hung greasily over his ears, a loose, very worn brown raincoat, dark trousers and unpolished black shoes. His hands were in his pockets.

If it had not been only two days before Christmas, and the

spirit of charity not been in the air, Andrew would probably have been prepared to say that he did not want to buy anything, or to have his car cleaned, or to discuss the Bible. He did not actually possess a car. To someone who lived in London, he believed, it was merely an encumbrance. He had arrived at Rockford the day before by train, and had been met at the station by Colin Cahill. And although he enjoyed reading the Bible, he preferred to discuss it only with intimates.

As it was, before he had said anything, the man had stated in a positive tone, "You're not Sir Lucas Dearden."

"That's correct," Andrew said. "I am not."

"I was told he lives here," the man said.

"He lives next door," Andrew replied.

Through the beech trees at the edge of the Cahills' garden, the old red brick of the Deardens' house was visible.

"They told me he lived down Stillmore Lane," the man said. "That's Stillmore Lane out there, isn't it?"

"Yes, I think that's what it's called," Andrew said.

The lane that passed the Deardens' and Cahills' houses, emerging on the village green of Upper Cullonden, was a very narrow one, so narrow that passing-bays had had to be carved out of the hedgerows to make it possible for any car to pass another. In the days of the horse, when there had been only the Deardens' house, and later the Cahills' small Victorian one (originally a vicarage), such things of course had not been necessary.

"I've rung and knocked next door," the man said, "and there's no answer."

"As a matter of fact, I believe Sir Lucas is in London," Andrew said, "but if the rest of the family aren't in I expect it's only because they've gone out shopping or something of the sort. Can I give them a message?"

The man looked down at his dusty shoes and with one foot began to trace a semicircle on the doorstep.

"He's in London, you say," he said. "Know when he'll be back?"

If it had not been for those unevenly spaced eyes, Andrew might not have begun to feel that it had been indiscreet of him to say even as much as he had. Sir Lucas Dearden was a retired Q.C., who had been notable in his day and who now lived with his son and a daughter-in-law in the house next door, but who happened, so Andrew believed, to be going to spend Christmas in London with a daughter and her husband.

"I'm afraid I've no idea," he said, though he was fairly sure that it was at the New Year that Sir Lucas intended to return. "But his son will be able to tell you."

"And you think he'll be in soon."

"I believe so."

"D'you think it'd be worth my while to wait for him?"

"I'm afraid I can't really say."

Andrew knew that he and the Cahills, and that included their son Jonathan who lived with them and would be home from his work in Rockford later in the day, were to have Christmas dinner with Nicholas and Gwen Dearden. But that was the day after tomorrow. What they might be doing now he truly did not know.

"Well, thanks," the man said, turning abruptly on his heel and walking away.

Andrew stood in the doorway, watching him. He appeared not to have come by car, for after pausing for a moment at the gate, looking towards the Deardens' house as if he were considering returning to it, he set off walking with long, weary-looking strides in the opposite direction along the lane towards the village. Not sure why he felt it, yet a little relieved to see him go, Andrew closed the door and returned to the washing-up.

Colin and Dorothea returned from their shopping a little before twelve o'clock.

Colin was about fifty, of medium height and of medium plumpness, not what could be called fat, but his bones were well covered. He had an oval face with a high forehead and a softly rounded chin, pink, rounded cheeks, and a full-lipped mouth which suggested that he would probably enjoy good food and drink. He was going slightly bald, though what was left of his hair was still a reddish brown. His eyes were large and bright blue. Dorothea had once assured Andrew that when Colin was young he had been very handsome. He did not find this impossible to believe, but thought that what Colin had probably had, rather than actual good looks, was a kind of cherubic charm. Only the intelligence in those big eyes suggested that within the cherub there must lurk someone thoughtful, observant and probably critical.

Dorothea was almost the same age as Colin, and at a first glance could be taken for a gentle little mouse of a woman. She was small, slender, fine-boned and very quiet in her movements. She had a small, pointed face, tanned to a soft, warm brown by all the time that she spent working in her garden, and shy, dark eyes and thick dark hair, usually rolled up in a rather dishevelled bun. But the mouselike impression that she gave could be dispelled in a moment if she suddenly exploded into speech. She was a natural chatterer about whatever happened to come into her head.

She and Colin were dressed almost alike in quilted anoraks, grey trousers and pullovers knitted by herself, hers a bright pink and his a dark blue.

"We've been buying up the town," she told Andrew. "Chocolates and crystallized fruits and Cointreau and smoked salmon and some cheeses, and a cold chicken for tonight and of course things for salads. What a mercy it is that I haven't got to bother about a Christmas dinner, because of course we should have had to have one if we weren't going to the Deardens'. Isn't it funny, we never buy chocolates or crystallized fruits or Cointreau for ourselves all the year round till we get to Christmas, yet we love them and could have them as often as we liked? Are you like that, Andrew? Are there treats you only allow yourself on very special occasions?"

She and Colin had put down their plastic shopping-bags in the kitchen and had gone into the sitting-room, where Colin started pouring out sherry. The room was of a fair size, with a high ceiling edged with an elaborate plaster cornice, a white marble fireplace—the grate of which had been filled in with an electric fire, now glowing redly, though central heating kept the room comfortably warm—tall windows and a door leading out onto a paved terrace. The easy chairs and the long sofa all looked somewhat the worse for wear, and were covered in faded flowered cretonne, but they were comfortable. The walls were lined with book-shelves filled with a disorderly collection of fine editions and paperbacks.

As they sat drinking their sherry Andrew presently remarked, "By the way, we had a visitor this morning. I don't know who he was, but he took a look at me and then assured me that I wasn't Sir Lucas Dearden. I agreed with him."

"Didn't he say who he was?" Colin asked.

"No, and didn't leave a message either," Andrew said. "He seemed to think perhaps the Deardens lived here. He said he'd been next door and couldn't get any answer. I told him I thought Sir Lucas was in London, then felt I ought not to have said it because he struck me as being perhaps a rather dubious character. But I said the family were sure to be home soon, in case he'd had any thought of breaking and entering."

"Really?" Dorothea said. She had sat down on the sofa and drawn her knees up to her chin, a habit she had which made her look very small and shrunken. "You really thought of that? What interesting things come into your mind, Andrew. I know you've had some contact with crime, but surely not at Christmas time and at Upper Cullonden. Which reminds me, I haven't put our decorations up yet. We've a holly in the garden which is simply loaded with berries. After lunch I'll go out and get some, just to tuck in over the pictures. I like Christmas to feel like Christmas, though as a matter of fact I never really do unless there are crackers and paper hats. That's left over from childhood. We used to have wonderful

Christmases when I was a child. Do you think there'll be crackers and paper hats at the Deardens'? I don't suppose there will. They've never had any children themselves and they'd think it was childish. But there'll be turkey and plum pudding, neither of which I actually like very much. I used to love turkey once upon a time. In those days it had some flavour. Now it mostly tastes like flannel. And I always liked ice cream better than plum pudding. But I like mince pies. I've made a good many for ourselves and we can have some tonight, unless you feel they ought to be kept until Christmas Eve."

"This man who came here," Colin said. "What was he like, Andrew?"

"Very tall and thin and rather shabby," Andrew answered. "A sort of air of being down on his luck."

"And he thought the Deardens lived here," Colin said.

"He didn't really seem to be sure where they lived."

"So he isn't anyone we know."

"So it appeared."

"Perhaps he was someone looking for a job or help of some kind."

"He could have been."

"Or someone out of Lucas's past," Dorothea suggested. "A criminal lawyer like Lucas might have had all sorts of strange connections."

"I don't know that the man was exactly strange," Andrew said. "Rather ordinary, actually."

"Haven't you seen pictures of the most outrageous criminals who look utterly ordinary?" she said. "And as it happens, Lucas is busy writing his memoirs. I suppose, being a lawyer, he'll know how to steer clear of libel, but all kinds of people may be in it. Someone like our visitor, for instance."

"Only he really didn't seem certain for a moment when he saw me that I wasn't Dearden," Andrew said. "He took a good look at me before he stated definitely that I wasn't. So he can't have known him well."

"You and Lucas aren't in the least alike," Dorothea said.

"Except in our ages."

"And you're about the same height."

"But certainly not as good-looking as he is."

"Oh, I can't help admitting that," she said and laughed. "You know, when he was young he must have been terrific. That fine aquiline nose, those chiselled lips, those beautiful eyebrows. In his wig he must have looked like something very special, straight out of the eighteenth century."

"In my opinion," Colin said, "he's probably more impressive now in old age than he was when he was younger. Some people are like that."

"You say he's writing his memoirs," Andrew said.

"Yes, I believe that's one of the things that's taken him to London," Dorothea said. "He's gone to talk things over with his agent. Then he's going on to stay over Christmas with Erica and Henry. Why don't you write your memoirs, Andrew? I'm sure you've had an interesting life."

"Everyone has had an interesting life," Andrew answered. "But making it interesting on paper is another matter. I've resolved never to try to do it. This increasing tendency in our population to live into the seventies and eighties must mean the market's flooded with memoirs from worthy old gentlemen. It must be almost as badly flooded as it is with children's stories, or anyway used to be. I don't know if it's still the case, but I believe there was a time when every woman who'd had a child and used to get it off to sleep with a bed-time story thought she could write the thing down for publication and make some money. But I've news for you. I've got a contract."

"You!" Dorothea exclaimed. "You don't mean you've finished your book on Robert Hooke?"

"Well . . ." Andrew hesitated. "Almost. Anyway, I've got a contract."

"I've never believed you'd finish that thing," Colin said.

That did not surprise Andrew. Ever since his retirement

he had been working on a biography of Robert Hooke, the
noted seventeenth-century microscopist, botanist and archi-
tect; a work which he had assumed when he started would
take him perhaps a year or so to complete had somehow
lasted until the present time. Even yet it was not quite finished. Apart from the fact that more research had been necessary than he had originally envisaged, he had developed a
habit of tearing up on one day what he had written the day
before. He was aware that to people who knew him inti-
mately the project had become something of a joke, so there
was something peculiarly satisfying about being able to tell
these friends that he had induced a publisher to give him a
contract for the almost, though not quite, completed work.

It was true that the publisher was the friend of a friend
and had only recently set up in business, but having a contract signed and put away safely—in the same drawer of his
desk at home where he kept his birth certificate, the certificate of his marriage, a copy of his will, the title deeds of his
flat in St. John's Wood and some share certificates—gave Andrew a feeling of satisfaction and security. It almost convinced him that one day he would really finish the book.

"But what on earth will you do with yourself when the
thing's published?" Dorothea asked.

"Oh, I've a number of ideas," Andrew said. "A biography
of Malpighi, for instance, another noted botanist. I'll definitely promise you, however, that I won't write my memoirs."

"Perhaps you're wise," she said. "But I know Lucas is very
proud of his. He's convinced himself it'll be a best seller. I
think Nicholas has done his best to discourage him so that he
won't be too disappointed if it flops. But Lucas has always
ridden roughshod over Nicholas. I've often wondered how
he and Gwen can really bear living with the old man. Nicholas is such a gentle creature, in spite of the violent stuff he
writes. And of course the house belongs to Lucas, and he's
got loads of money, and Nicholas may think it would be a

good thing to inherit it, even if he's making a reasonable sort of income now. It would be a sort of protection for Gwen, wouldn't it, if Nicholas happened to drop dead or if his public got tired of him, or anything like that happened? Anyway, money's always nice."

Nicholas Dearden was Sir Lucas's son and Gwen was his daughter-in-law. Nicholas had begun life by going into the law, but perhaps partly because he had felt that he would always be overshadowed by his brilliant father, he had not persevered in it, but had taken to writing spy stories, which had become moderately successful. He could have no pressing need for support from his father, and if he continued to live with the strong-willed, arrogant old man, it was more likely to be out of a sense of responsibility for the welfare of his aged parent than out of motives of greed.

"This man who came here this morning," Colin said, his mind apparently still held by the subject, "did he say if he was staying here?"

"He didn't say anything about himself," Andrew replied. "I'm sorry, perhaps I ought to have tried to find out a little more about him, but it simply didn't occur to me. My first thought was that he might be a Jehovah's Witness, or something like that."

"I don't suppose it matters," Colin said, "but I think I'll mention it to Nicholas."

"Why are you worried about him?" Andrew asked.

"Oh, I'm not worried." But there was a slight crease in Colin's high forehead, the faint indication of a frown, and a brooding look had come into his eyes, as if his mind were pursuing some thought that was at least mildly disturbing. "I think I heard of something . . . But it's nothing."

The frown faded and Colin devoted himself to refilling their glasses.

They had a lunch of bread and cheese, apples from the garden and coffee. Afterwards Andrew felt inclined to sleep, but he had been fighting off the tendency to let himself sleep in the afternoons, just as for some time he had been fighting against an inclination to get into pyjamas and a dressing-gown early in the evening. He knew that old age had him in its grasp, but he did not mean to yield to it too completely yet. He allowed himself to doze briefly in an armchair in the sitting-room, but then decided to set out for a walk.

He knew that Dorothea was in the garden, gathering the holly that she wanted for decorating the sitting-room, and he could hear the clicking of Colin's typewriter coming from upstairs. He was working on a paperback about the effect of radioactive compounds on vegetation. Andrew changed out of slippers into walking-shoes and set off down the garden path to the gate.

The day was mild and damp, with a gusty wind blowing and grey clouds moving erratically across the sky with only an occasional gleam of blue between them. There was a scent of moist earth in the air, and there were rotting beech leaves underfoot, blown down from the trees that separated the Cahills' garden from the Deardens'. There was certainly no possibility of a white Christmas this year unless the weather changed drastically in the next twenty-four hours. That was something for which Andrew was thankful. In his youth he had two or three times gone skiing in Switzerland, but snow in England he had always thought of as a very poor imitation of the real thing, bringing cold, damp and discomfort but lacking in entertainment value.

It could have its own beauty, of course, changing the whole visible world with its shining covering before traffic had churned it up and its whiteness had begun to disintegrate into slush, but at best it was a half-hearted affair. Andrew, soon after his retirement, had spent a Christmas in Australia, where the temperature had been a hundred degrees; and in spite of having just consumed with friends a large traditional meal of turkey and plum pudding, his afternoon had been spent swimming in a deliciously warm sea.

He thought of it now with nostalgia. That was really the kind of Christmas that he enjoyed. He was glad that today was mild, and that there were actually a few roses still in bloom in the garden.

In the lane he turned towards the village. He knew that if he went as far as the village green, skirted it, then took a turning to the left, he would find himself on the main road to Rockford. Although this was called a main road, it was really just a country road and never very busy, and if he proceeded along this for a mile or so he would find himself at the point where Stillmore Lane branched off it. So he could then return along it to the Cahills' house, making a circle of a length that just suited him.

On the side of the lane facing the two houses were allotments in which not much was growing at the moment but brussels sprouts and there were a few sheds dotted about where allotment holders kept their tools. But these were almost hidden from the lane by a high hedgerow, even though at present the hawthorns, the hazels, the briars and the occasional bush of elderberry growing along it were leafless. There were large puddles in the lane from rain that had fallen in the night. Andrew walked briskly, picking his way among them, glad that he had triumphed over the temptation to sleep.

As he went he found himself muttering a few lines of verse to himself. This was a bad habit he had, of which he could not break himself, although it irritated him intensely. As a child he had read poetry avidly, and he had had only to read some poem once or twice for it to become imprinted on his memory for life. At the moment it was a few lines of Scott that jingled in his mind.

> Heap on more wood!—the wind is chill;
> But let it whistle as it will,
> We'll keep our Christmas merry still . . .

"Marmion," wasn't it? Scott now was not one of his favourite poets. His taste had changed since his childhood. He would have been far happier murmuring some Shakespeare or Donne or Marvell. But just then, and he knew that it was likely to last for some days, he was Scott's victim.

Heap on more wood . . .

So it went on. He reached Upper Cullonden in about ten minutes. It was built around a triangular green with a pond in the middle, on which some domesticated-looking ducks cruised placidly. At the corner where the road to Rockford branched off there was a garage which was also a shop, selling newspapers and a modest supply of groceries. On the far side of the green there was a church with a square-built Norman tower and next to it an inn called The Running Man. Part of the inn was of lath and plaster, with a thatched roof, and no doubt dated at least from the fifteenth century, but an extension had been built onto it in recent times of the sort of harsh red brick that never weathers, and roofed with tiles. The inn advertised take-away fish and chips, sandwiches and hot pies. The rest of the village consisted of ancient cottages and recently built bungalows. A village hall, a post office, a school and another shop were dotted around the green. As Andrew approached he noticed a man emerge from the shop and walk towards The Running Man. He was tall, very thin, wearing a loose raincoat and a black beret.

Andrew stood still, looking after him. For an instant he felt an impulse to follow him, but as he disappeared into the pub this seemed to be a pointless thing to do. Even if he was the man who had called at the Cahills' house that morning, and Andrew was not even sure that he was, he had nothing to say to him about Sir Lucas Dearden, or any questions to ask him that might not be impertinent. He walked on along the road skirting the green and turned into the Rockford road.

It was about half past three when he got back to the

Cahills' house. Already there was a faint premonition of dusk in the air, and it felt a little colder than when he had set out. But as he pushed open the front door, which was usually locked only at night or when the house was left empty, he heard Colin's typewriter still clicking upstairs. In the sitting-room sprigs of holly, bright with berries, had been tucked along the tops of the picture frames, and in one corner of the room the bare branch of some fruit tree had been erected in a large bowl of earth and been hung all over with Christmas cards. It made a not unattractive substitute for a Christmas tree. Andrew could hear the radio in the kitchen, which told him that Dorothea was busy there. Even if Christmas dinner was to be eaten at the Deardens', it looked as if she intended to have some festivities here. If her son Jonathan had been ten years younger, no doubt she would have worked at it even harder.

Andrew had met Jonathan the evening before, though this morning he had left the house to go to his work in Rockford before Andrew had come down to breakfast. He was twenty-five and for the last three months had worked for a big construction firm, with a good salary, but he still lived at home. Andrew had known him since his childhood, or at least had met him often enough, when he visited the boy's parents, to feel that he knew him, though he had really very little knowledge of Jonathan's interests or abilities. He had taken a Top Second in economics, and then a Ph.D. at London University, but then instead of trying to enter on an academic career, as Andrew believed his parents had rather hoped, he had accepted the job that had been offered to him by the Rockford firm through the influence of a friend, and he seemed happy in it.

He was a cheerful, good-looking young man of medium height, well-built, with his father's oval face—though with a pointed chin rather than plump jowls—and with his father's reddish hair; of this, however, he still had plenty, tumbling in curls over a high, well-shaped forehead. His work seemed to be on the administrative rather than the practical side of the firm, and Andrew felt that at a fairly early age he might become a tolerably successful man. Andrew had always liked him, and he seemed to have a considerable affection for Andrew. He would probably get home from his work, as he had the day before, at about half past five.

After going upstairs to change his muddy shoes for slippers, Andrew returned to the sitting-room and sat down near to the glowing electric fire. He knew that in a little while Dorothea would bring in tea, a pleasure to which he never troubled to treat himself when he was alone at home, and he had no intention of falling asleep before she did so; but the warmth of the room after his walk almost at once brought on an attack of drowsiness, and it was with a start that he woke to become aware that she had just wheeled a tea-trolley in and had gone out into the hall to shout up to Colin that tea was ready.

The tapping of the typewriter ceased and Colin came downstairs.

Dorothea had been baking that afternoon, and there were hot scones dripping with butter and raspberry jam, and a sponge cake and some cucumber sandwiches of fabulous thinness.

"You know, I believe this is the only house where I'm still given cucumber sandwiches for tea," Andrew said. "When I was a child I used to be taken on a state visit sometime during every school holiday to an old aunt who was said to have lots of money, some of which my parents hoped she would leave to me, and it didn't matter what time of year it was, or what day in the week, but there were always cucumber sandwiches."

"And did she leave you any of her money?" Dorothea asked.

"A bit," Andrew said. "It helped to give me a fairly comfortable life while I was a student, but there wasn't as much as people thought and I had lots of cousins who all got their share too. And of course I got through it all long ago, and even if I hadn't it wouldn't be worth much now, what with inflation and all. But she was a nice old lady and I enjoyed the sandwiches and the cakes she used to have. By the way, Colin, when I was out for my walk I think I caught sight of our morning visitor, though I only had a glimpse of him, so I'm not really sure if it was the same man. He was going into that pub, The Running Man."

"Do you think he's staying there?" Colin asked. "They've two or three rooms that they let."

"I don't know," Andrew said. "Remembering how you seemed worried when I told you about him, I almost went after him to see if he'd tell me a bit more about why he came. But after all I didn't think it would be a particularly good idea."

"I'm not worried," Colin said, but again his forehead had a little crease on it. "It's just that Lucas once said something when some judge he knew died—that if he died too, a man whom he'd prosecuted, I believe for murder, and who got a life sentence, wouldn't have much left to live for when they eventually let him out. Apparently the man threatened both Lucas and the judge from the dock. And I understand he's free at last. It's funny, but I wasn't sure when Lucas talked about it that he wasn't a bit frightened, though he tried to turn it into a joke. However, I don't suppose he was really scared. And there's no reason to connect the man who came here with that murderer. All the same . . ."

"Yes?" Andrew said, as Colin paused.

Colin shook his head. "No, I just thought for a moment I'd stroll up to The Running Man after tea and see if he's there, and if so, what sort of character he seems to be. But there'd be no sense in it really. I could hardly go up to him and ask him straight out if he'd once done a murder."

"Whom did this man you're talking about murder?"

"His wife, I believe. That's the commonest sort of murder, isn't it? The domesticated kind. She'd been having an affair, or rather I think it was several, and the man got jealous and killed her. I believe it was thought he'd had plenty of provocation, so his sentence wasn't actually as long as it might have been, although it was called life. But the case seemed to have made a rather deep impression on Lucas. Perhaps he'd a certain sympathy for the man, even though he had to prosecute him."

"Do you think he's put an account of it in his memoirs?" Dorothea asked.

"Mightn't that be a rather dangerous thing to do from the point of view of libel?" Andrew said. "I mean if the man's out and about now."

"Yes, I shouldn't think Lucas would risk it," Colin replied. "But d'you know, I think I'll just wander up to The Running Man after all and see if he's there. I can say I've come to buy some whisky while I'm at it."

"Take the torch then," Dorothea said. "It's dark enough already and by the time you get back it'll be quite dark. I hope the battery doesn't pack up while you're out. It's some time since I got a new one."

"I won't need the torch," Colin said. "I know the way."

However, when he set out after the tea was finished, he did take the torch, the beam of which, as he shone it down the garden path towards the gate, cut a bright cone of light out of the early shadows of the evening. Because the clouds were low the darkness was deep, and because a gusty wind was still blowing, as it had been all day, the beech trees made their presence felt by moaning and sighing, although they were invisible. Beyond them Andrew, who had followed Colin to the front door, saw lights in the windows of the Deardens' house. So Nicholas and Gwen, wherever they had been that morning, had returned. He closed the door on Colin and went to the kitchen to help Dorothea wash up the tea things.

Colin was gone for about half an hour.

When he came into the sitting-room, where Andrew by

then had settled down to read a copy of *The Economist* he had found there, while Dorothea had begun cooking for the evening, Colin said, "No good, he wasn't there."

"You mean he isn't staying there?" Andrew asked.

"Yes, he is, he's taken a room for the night, but he happened to be out. And I found out his name. The landlord, Joe Hobson, is always ready to gossip. It's Thomas Waterman."

"And does that ring a bell?"

"I've a sort of feeling it does."

"You mean he really could be this murderer you were talking about?"

"Oh, I can't say that for sure. I'd have to look it up. But I can tell Lucas, when he comes home, that a man called Thomas Waterman has been inquiring for him, and it may mean something to him. Now I'm ready for a drink. What about you?"

Andrew said that as usual he was ready for one, and Colin again poured out three glasses of sherry. Dorothea came from the kitchen to join them.

She settled herself on the sofa in her favourite position, in a small ball with her knees up to her chin.

"Jonathan will soon be home," she said. "He's got to go to work tomorrow, but of course he's got Christmas Day and Boxing Day off, and the day after too, and that gets us to Saturday and then of course there's Sunday, so really he'll be free for a number of days. That's nice, isn't it? Not that much will be going on at his office until after the New Year. What do you think, Andrew, do you think it's a good thing for him to go on living with us here instead of his finding somewhere for himself in Rockford and being independent?"

"I shouldn't think you interfere much with his independence," Andrew said.

"Oh, we don't, and of course it's much more economical for him to live with us than to pay rent for a flat of his own," she said. "But what did you do when you were his age? Did you live with your parents?"

"No, though that wasn't because I'd have minded doing so," Andrew replied. "But it happened that they lived in Devon and I was a student in London. Then I got a job in the Midlands and I got married, so as a matter of course I moved out from my old home."

"Well, Jonathan was away from home while he was in London at University," Dorothea said, "and he seemed quite happy about that. But we're more than delighted to have him here now. Actually it's marvellous for us. And I think he's contented. It's just that I feel perhaps he ought to want to get free of us. Isn't that an important part of growing up? I sometimes think there must be something immature about him if he wants to stay here."

"That isn't how he struck me yesterday evening," Andrew said. He always became uneasy when people, who after all could only be amateurs, tried to explore the complexities of psychology.

"If you ask me, I think he's mature enough to recognize that rent-free accommodation has its advantages," Colin said, with a slightly wry smile.

"That's horrid of you!" Dorothea exclaimed. "He pays his share, doesn't he? He's insisted on doing that ever since he got his job. It's only that I can't help wondering . . ."

But what she could not help wondering was never stated, for at that moment an enormous noise shattered the quiet of the winter evening. The banging and shrieking of metal against metal, as well as several fearful thuds, made up the roaring sound of a terrible explosion.

"God!" Colin cried out, starting up from his chair. "That isn't thunder, is it? It sounded just like a bomb."

Andrew had been in a fire brigade in the war during the blitz on London.

"It was a bomb," he said.

TWO

AS THEY RACED FOR THE DOOR Colin snatched up
the torch that he had carried out when he went out earlier in
the evening. But there was no need for it. The garden was lit
up by a leaping red light of the flames from a blazing car in
the lane. It was a little beyond the Deardens' gate. Most of
the car had been blown to fragments, though the main body
of it was intact and was the heart of the fire. A figure, or what
might once have been a figure, was curved horribly over
what might once have been the steering-wheel. But lumps of
metal, shreds of glass and a tyre had been flung up into the
hedge and scattered on the ground.

"Jonathan!" Dorothea shrieked as the three of them ran on
till the heat from the blazing wreck stopped them.

Colin was in the lead, and he spread out his arms so that
she could not pass him.

"It isn't Jonathan's car," he shouted above the roaring of
the flames.

She only cried out again in terror, "Jonathan!"

"No!" Colin shouted back.

Other figures were running out from the Deardens' house. As the fierce illumination of the fire fell upon them Andrew recognized Nicholas Dearden and his wife Gwen. There was a third figure a little behind them, a woman, but Andrew did not pay much attention to her. It was no one he knew. Nicholas was the first to reach the gate, but only just outside it he stood still, raising an arm to shield his face from the heat.

"It's Dad!" he shouted.

His wife came to his side, her face looking strangely white in spite of the red light that fell on it.

"He's in London!" she yelled.

"It's Dad!" Nicholas repeated. "It's his car. We want the fire brigade!"

He turned and raced for the house.

"Water! The hose—we've got a garden hose!" Gwen cried.

"It won't help," Colin said. He went to her side and put an arm round her shoulders. "It's too late to do anything. By the time the fire brigade gets here it'll have burnt itself out."

"But look!" she called out wildly. "Our windows! It was a bomb—a bomb here in Stillmore Lane. Look, it's smashed all our windows!"

Andrew looked at the house—a dignified, peaceful-looking Georgian house—and saw that indeed several of the windows had been shattered.

Dorothea was crying, less for the sake of the man who had been hideously blasted to death than from relief that he was not Jonathan.

"The police," Colin said. "They'll be wanted as well as the fire brigade."

He turned and ran after Nicholas into the house.

The woman who had come out of the house behind Nicholas and Gwen moved up to Gwen's side.

"We can't do anything here," she said. "Come inside."

But she must have known, as Andrew did, that Gwen would not respond. Though it was true that there was noth-

ing that any of them could do near to the blazing car and its
slaughtered occupant, to turn and go away and leave it was
impossible. He himself felt rooted to where he stood by some
powerful though obviously irrational sense of responsibility.

The spell was broken by Nicholas and Colin re-emerging
from the house.

"You'd better go in," Nicholas said. "I'll wait here till the
fire brigade arrives."

He was a small man of about thirty-five with a shock of fair
hair and features that were not unlike his handsome father's,
though a softened, blurred version of them. His nose was less
sharp, his mouth wider and less finely formed, his eyebrows
shaggier. He was dressed in corduroy trousers and a cardigan. For the moment his voice was shaky, and there was an
indecisiveness in his movements, though he was trying hard
to assume an air of authority.

"Yes, go on, go in," Colin said. "I'll wait here with Nicholas."

"But Jonathan!" Dorothea wailed. "He'll be along any
minute now. He won't be able to get past."

"I should think he'll have the sense to back into one of the
passing-bays," Colin said.

It struck Andrew that Colin was the calmest person there,
except perhaps for the woman who was standing next to
Gwen. Because of the horror inside him he was not aware of
how calm he looked himself.

"Yes, come in," the woman said.

Gwen allowed herself to be led slowly towards the house.
She kept glancing back over her shoulder at the fire. She was
about the same height as her husband, but about five years
younger. She wore jeans and a sweater, and her dark hair was
long and hung in a thick plait down her back. Her face was
small and pointed and, as Andrew remembered from earlier
meetings with her, was always pale, though when it was not
distorted by shock, as it was now, it had a delicate kind of
charm.

Andrew hesitated, not sure if he should follow her into the house or if he should stay in the lane with the two men, but then Dorothea took his arm and drew him after Gwen. The unknown woman followed them.

In the light that was on in the hall he saw that she was taller than either of the Deardens, slender and probably about thirty, which meant that she was about the same age as Gwen. She had soft fair hair, cut short and curling loosely about a small, well-shaped head. Her eyes were grey and full of concentration. She was wearing a very plain grey dress which might have looked severe if it had not been for a necklace of mixed chains of gold and silver round her neck. But even it had a certain look of restraint about it.

Gwen led the way into the drawing-room, a high room which would have been splendid if the furniture in it had looked as if it belonged there. But most of it looked as if it had arrived from Scandinavia not very long ago. It was all pale and angular. The easy chairs had arms of stainless steel and were covered in some black plastic material. Some alarming abstract paintings hung on the walls. Andrew, who had been in the room before, tried to convince himself that the uneasiness he felt in it was merely the result of old-fashioned prejudice and should not be yielded to; yet he still felt that its cool, sharp-edged neatness was somehow hostile to someone like himself. But at least its windows, which looked out onto the garden behind the house, had not been blown in by the bomb blast like those in the front of the house.

Dorothea immediately became busy in one of her silent, mouse-like bouts of activity, going from cupboard to cupboard, obviously searching for something, though it had not been suggested that she should do this. Gwen dropped into a chair, and hid her face in her hands. Her whole body was shaking.

The unknown woman turned to Andrew and said, "I'm Lyn Goddard, an old friend of Gwen's. I arrived this morning. I'm staying for Christmas."

"I'm Andrew Basnett," he replied. "I arrived yesterday and I'm also staying for Christmas."

"Ah, the professor," she said. "I've heard about you."

Gwen suddenly jerked upright in her chair, dropping her hands from her face, and shrieked, "For God's sake, what are you looking for, Dorothea?"

"Brandy," Dorothea answered.

"It's in the dining-room," Lyn Goddard said. She had a soft yet deep-voiced way of speaking. "I know where it is. I'll get it."

"I don't want any brandy," Gwen said. "You have it, if you want it."

"You may find it'll help," Lyn Goddard said. She went out of the room.

"It can't be Dad in that car," Gwen stated on a high, hysterical note. "He's in London. He's spending Christmas with Erica and Henry."

"Was it his car?" Andrew asked.

"I don't know. How could anyone tell? A wreck like that— it could have been anybody's."

"You aren't sure?"

"No, I tell you! How could I be?"

"And you weren't expecting him home?"

"No, definitely not. He isn't coming home till next Monday."

"Yet your husband seemed sure."

"Perhaps he's right then. Perhaps it's Dad. But it doesn't make sense."

Lyn Goddard returned to the room, carrying a tray with a bottle and glasses on it. Without asking anyone if they wanted the brandy, she filled four glasses and gave one to each of the people there.

Dorothea took hers, found a couch on which she could sit with her feet up, and said, "Was it a bomb?"

"Unless the car exploded of its own accord," Lyn said. "I don't know if that's possible."

"A bomb that someone attached to Lucas's car in London," Dorothea said, "knowing that he was coming home. No, that can't be right, because if it had had a timing device it surely wouldn't have been set for so long ahead. I mean, he almost got home, didn't he? If it had been a time-bomb they'd have set it to go off almost as soon as he got into the car. Or perhaps it would have gone off as soon as he started the engine."

"People sometimes make mistakes," Andrew said.

"What a lot you all seem to know about bombs," Gwen said bitterly.

"How can you help it if you watch the television news?" Dorothea sipped some brandy, which produced a sudden sharp shudder in her. "It's fearful for you, Gwen, I know that it is, because for a moment I thought, I really thought it was Jonathan. And I can't help feeling an awful callous sort of thankfulness that it isn't. I'm terribly sorry."

"It's Nicholas I'm really sorry for," Gwen said. Now that she had her glass of brandy, she was gulping rapidly and it seemed to steady her. "His mother died when he was so young that his father meant everything to him. That was why we had to live with him. Well, I don't mean we had to, but Nicholas always felt it was his duty—no, I don't mean duty, that sounds so cold—but anyway he felt it was up to him to look after him when he got old. Erica never did anything much for him. I was surprised when he decided to go and spend Christmas with her and Henry. And if it really is Dad . . ." She stopped.

"You were going to say, someone will have to tell them," Lyn said. "I'd leave that to Nicholas."

"Yes, of course. I wonder if there was a quarrel and that's why he suddenly came home."

"Is that likely?" Lyn asked.

"Perhaps—no— How can I know about a thing like that?" Gwen said feverishly. "Dad sometimes got furious with people for no special reason, but it always blew over quite quickly, especially if they said they were sorry, and Henry always did that, even if Erica didn't. Henry's always gone for a quiet life."

Andrew was beginning to feel that Gwen's affection for her father-in-law did not go very deep, and that what was really upsetting her, leaving her white-faced and slightly shaking, was the outrage of a bomb going off in Stillmore Lane. It upset him too, considerably. He shrank from his memory of the dark curved form that might have been a man hanging helplessly over the steering-wheel of the blazing car.

It seemed to be only a few minutes later that they heard the wailing of the fire-brigade siren. Andrew finished his brandy, refused the refill that Lyn immediately offered him and went out of the house towards the gate. In the garden it had become what felt very dark and quiet, though the flames in the lane had not quite died down. But their roaring had ceased.

He saw Nicholas and Colin standing just outside the gate. Men in helmets and overalls, holding what Andrew supposed were fire extinguishers, squirted foam over what was left of the fire, moving rapidly about in its flickering light. He could see clearly now the blackened figure of a man in the car.

In the distance the wailing of another siren had just become audible.

"That'll be the police," Colin said.

"Is it—" Andrew began hesitatingly.

"Is it Lucas?" Colin said. "It's his car."

"Yes, it's my father," Nicholas said.

"You can't be sure, can you?" To Andrew the figure at the wheel seemed unidentifiable.

"Yes, it's him." Nicholas did not look at Andrew when he spoke, but kept a hard, bright gaze fixed on the car. His pleasant, sensitive face looked strangely empty. "But he was dead already when we came out, wasn't he? We couldn't have done anything to help him."

"No, you certainly couldn't have," Colin said. He had not

lost his composed, faintly cherubic look even when gazing at the corpse. It might have been thought that he had spent his life looking at such scenes.

"If we'd come out faster . . ." Nicholas's voice faded.

"No, if it was a bomb he'd have been killed instantaneously."

"Have the fire-brigade men said it was a bomb?" Andrew asked.

"No, I think they're leaving that to the police, but it couldn't have been anything else." A look of extreme weariness had come over Nicholas. His shoulders had slumped and all of a sudden he turned his back on the car, as if he could not bear to go on looking at it. "I'll have to tell Erica. Why don't you two go in? I'll stay here till the police arrive, but there's no need for you to stay."

"It's all right, we'll stay here," Colin said. "But how will the police get along the lane?"

The burning car filled it. No car could have passed. The fire-brigade men had managed to reach the wreck by forcing their way into the hedgerows on either side of it. The fire engine was a little way down the lane beyond it.

"The same way as these men did," Nicholas said, "but they'll have to leave their car some way back. Thank God at least we're spared sightseers."

That, Andrew was ready to admit, was one advantage of living in as isolated a spot as this. Virtually no traffic came along the lane except to the two houses.

The wailing of the police siren grew louder. A moment later, as a white and blue car appeared beyond the fire engine, the sound stopped. There was a pause, then four men came scrambling along, fighting their way through the charred hawthorns and hazels, till they came face to face with Nicholas, who had turned to meet them.

"Mr. Dearden?" one of the men asked.

"Yes," Nicholas said.

"I'm Detective Chief Inspector Roland." The man, who was in plain clothes, was tall and broad-shouldered and heavy in his build. Though he could not have been much over forty his short, rough hair was grey. He had a square face with wide-spaced, heavy-lidded eyes. "It was you who telephoned?"

"Yes," Nicholas said.

"And that poor chap in there is your father?"

"Yes."

"You're sure? He isn't exactly recognizable."

"Yes, I'm sure."

"Is it his car?"

"Yes."

The car, Andrew had decided, was a Mercedes, though what colour it had been was impossible to tell.

"Did you see it happen?" the detective asked.

"No," Nicholas said. Then he turned to Colin and Andrew. "This is my next-door neighbour, Mr. Cahill, and a friend of his, Professor Basnett."

"And none of you saw anything?"

"We were all indoors," Colin said. "We only heard it."

"A loud noise?"

"Very loud."

"Did you see anybody in the lane when you came out?"

"Nobody."

"It isn't that I'd expect it, but one's got to ask." The inspector looked towards the other men who had come with him. They were standing near the car, watching the remains of the blaze with what looked almost like a stolid lack of interest. Perhaps they had seen other things like it before. One, like the inspector, was in plain clothes, the other two were in uniform. "And that's where you live?" he said to Nicholas, nodding towards the Deardens' house.

"Yes," Nicholas said again. It was almost as if he had lost the power of saying anything else.

"Well, I think it would be best if you'd go in while we have a look round, then I'll come in and get a few facts from you.

There's an ambulance coming, but it's obvious there's nothing they can do."

Except remove a corpse, Andrew thought, though the Inspector did not put this into words.

When the three men reached the drawing-room, Lyn Goddard went out and returned with more glasses, and gave them brandy without asking if they wanted it. Andrew was not sure that he did. The brandy that he had drunk before he went out was still coursing warmly through his blood. But he did not refuse it. Nicholas went to Gwen, put a hand on her shoulder and bent to kiss her.

"It's him?" she said. "It *is?*"

"I'm afraid so," he said.

"But why was he here?" she said. "He ought to have been with Erica and Henry."

"I know, and I'll have to telephone them to tell them what's happened," he said. "Perhaps they'll be able to explain it."

He moved towards the telephone.

"You could do it from the other room," she said.

He appeared not to hear her. He gave the impression of being lost to what was happening around him. He picked up the telephone and dialled. Everyone else in the room was silent.

After a moment he said, "Henry? Nicholas. A frightful thing— *What?*"

It seemed that he had been interrupted. It was a little while before he went on. "Today, you say? This morning? . . . Yes, yes, of course, I understand, but where . . . ? It's difficult to take in after what's happened here. Is she badly hurt? . . . Well, thank God for that . . . St. Raphael's, that's a private place, isn't it? And they think it'll be only a week or so? . . . I'm sorry, very sorry, Henry . . . No, I didn't know anything about it, because, you see, he never got here. That's to say, well, he did get here almost, but there seems to have been a bomb or something in his car, or in the lane or somewhere, and it went off just before he reached us and the car went up in flames and he's dead . . . Yes, *dead*, no question of it. The police are here and the fire brigade and an ambulance . . . I don't know, Henry, I think he was killed instantly, which is something to be thankful for . . ." There was another longish pause while the sound of the other voice on the telephone could be faintly heard in the room. Then Nicholas went on, "Yes, I see. Yes, naturally. It was probably the best thing to do. But who knew he was going to do it, Henry? That's the question I'd like answered at the moment. Did he see anyone in London besides you and Erica? . . . Yes, yes, the police, of course, but no one else that you know of? . . . Yes, it's an appalling thing and I'll keep in touch and tell you what happens. And you'll tell Erica when she's fit to be told, and give her our love."

He put the telephone down. Turning back to the room, he thrust his hand through his shock of fair hair, clawing it back from his forehead.

"Erica was in a car smash this morning," he said. "It happened quite near their home. A motor-cyclist tried to get ahead of her at the lights and she swerved to avoid him and was hit by a bus. She isn't badly hurt—well, not seriously. She's got two broken ribs and a damaged collar-bone and a good many cuts on her face from glass from the smashed windscreen, but she'll be all right. She was just going out shopping when this maniac tried to get past her. And that's why Dad didn't stay in London. She's in hospital, of course, that's to say a private place near them called St. Raphael's, which I believe is very good, and Henry's alone in their flat and Dad didn't think he could do any good by staying there, so he came home. But why he didn't let us know . . . ?" He paused and took the glass of brandy that Lyn held out to him.

"Perhaps he took for granted Henry would do that," she said. "And he may have been too shocked to think of doing it."

"Yes, that must be it," Nicholas said. "Henry seemed a bit

surprised that I didn't know of it. And I'm not sure if he's really taken in what I told him about what's happened here. I can't say I have myself yet."

"And did Dad really see no one in London but Henry and Erica?" Gwen asked.

"So Henry says. That's to say, they both saw the police who were handling Erica's accident, and the ambulance people, but that's all. Dad didn't even see his agent, whom he was going to see today. When he got to London yesterday the three of them went out to dinner together, then they went back to the flat and they didn't meet anyone they knew, and anyway, Erica's accident hadn't happened yet, so Dad hadn't any thought of coming home. He didn't decide to do that until after she was taken to the hospital."

"But someone must have known he was coming," Gwen said.

"And just about when too," Andrew observed.

He was thinking that a less self-centred man than Sir Lucas Dearden might have stayed with Henry Haslam to bear him company while he was becoming used to the thought of his wife's accident, even if perhaps he would have been less comfortable without his daughter there to look after him; if Lucas had done this he might have saved his own life.

The doorbell rang.

"The police," Colin said. He had sat down on the sofa beside Dorothea.

But it was not the police; it was Jonathan Cahill.

He had a slightly dishevelled look, with some scraps of charred twig clinging to the jacket of the dark suit that he wore to work. His hair was wind-blown and he had a scratch down one side of his face, which had a bewildered look of shock.

"What the hell's been going on?" he asked.

Dorothea jumped up from her chair, went to him and put her arms round him.

"Oh, Jonathan, when I first saw it I thought it was you!" she cried.

"How could it have been me, I don't drive a Mercedes," he said. He seemed to want to free himself from her embrace.

"But how did you get here?" she asked. "Did the police let you through?"

"Yes, of course," he said. "They wanted to know who I was and told me you were all in here, and I scrambled along the hedge past the wreck. Nicholas, I'm bloody sorry about it. It's your father, isn't it?"

"Didn't the police tell you that?" Nicholas asked.

"One of them did, as a matter of fact. They were just getting him—his body—out of the car, what's left of it, and taking it to an ambulance. But what happened? How did the car go on fire?"

"We don't know," Nicholas said, "except that there was a violent bang that sounded like a bomb, and when we got outside the car was in flames."

"What have you done with your car?" Dorothea asked.

"Backed it into one of the passing-bays when I saw the road ahead was blocked," Jonathan answered.

"Is the fire out yet?" Lyn asked.

He seemed to become aware of her presence for the first time. It appeared that he knew her. "Hallo, Lyn," he said. "When did you get here?"

"This morning," she answered, and repeated, "Is the fire out?"

"Just about," Jonathan answered. "But you aren't serious, are you, Nicholas? It couldn't have been a bomb."

"We won't really be sure till the police tell us," Nicholas said. "But it's unusual, I believe, for a car to explode of its own accord."

"Who'd want to do that to him?"

"Do any of us know who our enemies are?" Colin asked.

"Oh, I do, I certainly do," Jonathan said. He mopped at the

scratch on his face. "But I don't really expect even the worst of them to get around to murdering me."

"Unless one of them's insane," his father said. "You can't predict what they'll do then, even if you think you know them well. What have you done to your face?"

"I think it was the remains of a briar in the hedge, when I was getting past the car," Jonathan said. "It isn't anything. Have we all got to wait here for the police?"

"I think they expect it," Nicholas said.

"It's only that I thought we must be awfully in the way." Jonathan accepted the drink that Lyn brought him. "Did you drive down?" he asked her.

"No, I came by train," she said, "writing the Christmas cards that I ought to have done days ago and which are all going to arrive days late. Mine nearly always do. I make good resolutions about getting them off early every year, and then just forget them." She seemed to want to bring a note of normality into the talk in the room. A mistake, Andrew thought. Nothing could make it normal. "Gwen and Nicholas met me at the station."

That explained to Andrew why the house next door had been empty when Thomas Waterman called in the morning.

"Perhaps we really are in the way," Dorothea said. "I expect you'd all much sooner be alone. You've this worry about Erica too. You don't know about that, Jonathan. Erica was in a car crash this morning and she's in hospital. Luckily not too badly hurt."

"No, no, please don't go," Gwen said. "I can't give you much to eat, but I could make some sandwiches."

"I doubt if anyone's hungry," Colin said.

"And I should think you ought to stay until the police say if they want you here or not," Nicholas said. "They may want us all here."

Detective Inspector Roland presently arrived, accompanied by the other man in plain clothes whom they had all seen in the lane, and whom the inspector introduced as

Detective Sergeant Porter; a short, very wide man with a wide, bland face, he had the somewhat surprising look of appearing to think that he was on a pleasant social visit. It turned out that it would suit the inspector if the Cahills and Andrew returned to the house next door, so that he had not quite such a roomful of people to deal with all at once. He said that he would call on them shortly, though he understood that they might have seen nothing until after the explosion of the bomb.

"So you're sure it was a bomb," Colin said as they got up to go.

"Call it a land-mine," the inspector said. "But we're not a hundred percent sure. We'll have to wait till our experts get on to the job for that. But it's the assumption on which we're working at the moment."

Colin, Dorothea, Jonathan and Andrew left after Dorothea had told Gwen that she should call them immediately if there was any way in which they could help. They went out into the evening, which had become much darker than when they had come in, the flames from what was left of the wrecked car having died. Colin was still carrying the torch that he had brought with him. He switched it on and turned it towards the car and it showed the figures of the two uniformed men standing in the lane, talking. The fire engine and the ambulance had gone, and so had the crouching figure that had been visible in the car. There was a heavy smell of burning in the air and the hedgerows on both sides of the lane were blackened.

They walked in silence to the house next door with Colin leading the way and Dorothea clinging to Jonathan's arm, as if she were still not quite sure that he might somehow be lost to her if she did not keep a tight hold of him.

In the sitting-room they found the electric fire on, as they had left it, and the remains of the drinks on which they had started before the noise of the explosion had sent them racing out. After the brandy they had been drinking, the sherry did not seem very inviting, but Jonathan poured out a glass for himself.

"I don't understand," he said. "I thought old Lucas was in London."

Colin told him about Erica's accident and the reason for Lucas Dearden's return home.

"Good Lord!" Jonathan muttered. "Good Lord!" He drank some sherry. "But who knew he was coming home? Someone must have known if—well, if they intended to murder him."

"Or any of the rest of us," Colin said. "Or perhaps no one in particular. Vandalism on a peculiarly gruesome scale."

"Is that what you really think?" Jonathan asked. "A bomb just left in the lane as a sort of hideous joke for anyone who came along to run over?"

"No, as a matter of fact, I don't," Colin answered. "I think it was very deliberately aimed at Lucas. Andrew, what do you think?"

"He does seem somehow the most murderable of the people who live down this way," Andrew said.

"But someone did know he was coming," Jonathan insisted.

"Henry knew he was," Dorothea said.

"But Henry happens to be in London," Colin reminded her.

"But he could have telephoned . . . Oh, I didn't mean to say that!" she cried. "I almost said he could have telephoned them next door, or for that matter Lucas himself could have done that, but of course I didn't mean that. I'll tell you what I think happened. I think someone who didn't know he'd gone away planted the bomb, someone who perhaps saw him drive off this morning— No, that won't do, he drove off yesterday. So Jonathan's right, someone knew he was coming back, but didn't know Jonathan would be driving along the lane so soon after him and could as easily have been blown up in his car as Lucas was. And that doesn't sound like any of the Deardens, does it, though they all knew just about when Jon-

HUNTINGTON CITY-TOWNSHIP
PUBLIC LIBRARY
200 West Market Street
Huntington, IN 46750

athan came home. I wonder . . ." She paused in her hurrying speech. "Suppose Lucas had someone in the car with
him, someone who was armed with a bomb, and when Lucas
slowed down as he was getting near his gate, the man jumped
out, hurled the bomb at the car and bolted. Not one of us
looked at the allotments when we came out, did we? He
might have been running away across them without our seeing him."

"As a matter of fact, that makes rather good sense," Jonathan said in a slightly surprised tone, as if he were not accustomed to hearing sense from his mother. "Actually I think
the police thought of it themselves, because when I arrived
those two men we saw in the lane just now were going from
one tool-shed to the other and taking a look inside them all.
Not that this man, if there was one, wouldn't be miles away
by now. He'd probably have a car stashed somewhere. Mum,
what are we going to eat?"

He was young enough to be hungry in spite of what had
happened.

Dorothea gave a deep sigh, as if for once she found it difficult to think about providing food, which normally was at
the forefront of her mind.

"There's a cold chicken," she said, "and some salad, of
course, and a lot of mince pies, though I really meant to keep
them for tomorrow."

" 'God rest you merry, gentlemen, let nothing you dis-
may . . .' " Jonathan sang, half under his breath. "Well, we
shall have no carol singers this year, not even the Salvation
Army. They'll hardly think it appropriate to stand just out
there and sing. I'll miss them."

"I'm sorry, Dorothea, but I couldn't face a mince pie just
now," Andrew said. "Chicken only, please, and a very small
piece at that."

"Oh dear, Andrew, it's so awful to have brought you down
here for this," she said. "Just think, if you'd stayed at home
you could be sitting comfortably by your fire, just watching

the splendid sort of horrors that happen on television, and eating something nice from Marks and Spencer's, without a care in the world. I'm really sorry." She swallowed her sherry at a gulp, looked a little astonished that she had done so and went out to the kitchen.

Andrew admitted to himself, though he would not have done so to anyone else, that what she had said had entered his own mind. The lonely life that he led now, often meeting friends yet seldom anyone with whom he was truly intimate, had perhaps made him selfish, too concerned with his own comfort, as he had really not much else to live for. But he was trying to keep the deep desire to be in his own home well to the back of his mind.

"I'm only afraid I may be in the way," he said hypocritically. "I don't see how I can help, hardly knowing the Deardens."

"I think you can help us," Colin said, "just by being around. It may be useful having someone here who's detached from the whole situation. If any of us start to get hysterical, you can calm us down."

"But look!" Jonathan broke in. "Someone knew the old man was coming down. We're agreed on that. And it must have been someone here. He himself or Henry must have telephoned someone . . . No, I'm getting as bad as Mum. I don't mean any of the Deardens. All the same, someone knew."

That was what the police plainly believed, as appeared when Inspector Roland and Sergeant Porter arrived at the house about an hour later. By then Dorothea had produced a meal of cold chicken, salad and tinned apricots with some cream that she happened to have in the refrigerator. At first no one except Jonathan had wanted to eat, but she had insisted that it was very important to keep up one's strength at a time of stress, and everyone had managed to consume a small amount, though this was probably more in obedience to her authority than from any desire for food. Jonathan, helped by Andrew, was doing the washing-up when the police arrived.

They were offered drinks, refused them and sat down with the Cahills and Andrew in the sitting-room, the washing-up having been left only half finished.

"I believe you heard the bomb and were on the scene as soon as Mr. and Mrs. Dearden," Inspector Roland said. The heavy-lidded eyes in his square face moved from one to another of the people there, but seemed to say very little. They did not even show much curiosity.

"So it really was a bomb, was it?" Colin said.

"An explosive device of some sort, planted in the road," Roland said. "The area's roped off now, and if any traffic tries to come along the lane to Upper Cullonden it'll be turned off at the road junction."

"There won't be any traffic," Colin said. "Hardly anything comes here except to these two houses."

"I'll have to go and collect my car sometime," Jonathan said. "I can back it down the lane and drive round here by the village."

"It's your car, is it, the one in the lay-by?" Roland asked.

"Yes, I backed it in there when I saw the way ahead was blocked," Jonathan answered.

"But you were expected here, were you?" Roland said.

"Oh yes, it's just about my usual time for coming home," Jonathan said. "I work in Rockford, but I live here."

Roland turned back to Colin. "Did you go straight out as soon as you heard the bang?"

"Yes," Colin said.

"But I understand you didn't see anyone in the lane, either someone you might have expected to see, or some stranger?"

"No one at all."

"Did you happen to look at the allotments?"

"I don't think I did, no."

"Did any of you?"

He was answered by some muttered negatives.

"In any case," Colin said, "if there'd been someone there it would have been too dark to see him."

"Even with the flames from the fire lighting things up?"

"I think so, yes."

"And none of you knew that Sir Lucas was expected home? You had no telephone call from him or his son-in-law and then happened to mention it to someone?"

"As a matter of fact . . ." Andrew said and stopped.

"Yes?" Roland's incurious gaze settled on his face.

"It isn't that I knew anything about Sir Lucas coming home," Andrew said. "But there's something perhaps I ought to mention. In the morning when I was alone here while Mr. and Mrs. Cahill were out shopping, a visitor called. For a moment he seemed to think I might be Sir Lucas, then he came to the conclusion that I wasn't and he asked where Sir Lucas was, as he'd been told he lived here. I told him that Sir Lucas lived next door but that he was in London and I didn't know when he'd be back, and the man went away. I began to feel for some reason that I ought not to have said even as much as I had, but I didn't think much about it. Then in the afternoon I went for a walk along to the village and home again by the main road, and when I was in the village I think I saw this man going into that pub there, The Running Man. But I didn't go after him and try to speak to him or anything of the kind, and I can't tell you anything more about him. I'm only telling you this because I think you may be interested in any strangers who are interested in Sir Lucas who happen to be around at the moment."

"But I went to the pub later," Colin said quickly. "And this man, at least I presume it was the same man, had booked a room there for the night, though he wasn't there when I called in. But the landlord told me his name was Thomas Waterman."

For a moment the inspector's eyelids lifted and he said, "Waterman!"

"Didn't a Thomas Waterman commit a murder some years

ago?" Colin asked. "And didn't Lucas Dearden prosecute him?"

Roland said nothing. He folded his big hands over his stomach and gazed down at them. Sergeant Porter smiled as if someone at a party of some kind had just made a particularly good joke.

Jonathan seemed to have been getting restive. He leant forward in his chair.

"But still, even if this man Waterman planted the bomb," he said, "he'd have had to know when Lucas was coming. But he could have, you know. Once he knew Lucas was in London, he could have guessed he'd be with Henry and Erica. If he knew anything about the family, that is, and perhaps he did, he might have rung them up to say he wanted to meet Lucas or something, and been told he could meet him here if he waited. And so he waited, armed with his bomb, at the end of the lane where Lucas was sure to pick him up . . ."

He stopped, for just then the doorbell rang.

It was Lyn Goddard. She had no overcoat on and though the evening for the time of year was mild, she looked chilled. Dorothea tried to draw her towards the fire, but she resisted it.

"I'm sorry," she said, "I didn't mean to interrupt. But I wondered, Dorothea, if you could come back with me. Gwen's got quite hysterical. I can't do anything with her, and if Nicholas goes anywhere near her she screams. I thought perhaps you could help."

Dorothea looked at Roland. "Is it all right for me to go?"

"Yes, yes, of course," he said. "Must have been a terrible shock for the poor lady. But am I right that she's Sir Lucas's daughter-in-law, not daughter?"

"That's right," Colin said.

"His daughter is Mrs. Haslam, who's been in an accident in London, is that it?" Roland said. "That's what I understood from Mr. Dearden."

Colin nodded.

"But you came down from London this morning, Miss Goddard?" Roland went on.

"Yes, I told you so," she said.

"It's just that there's a question I'd like to ask you," he said. "Probably of no importance." It was the first time that Andrew noticed how often Inspector Roland asked questions which he insisted were of no importance. "Since you arrived next door, have there been any telephone calls?"

"I don't think so," she said.

"Ah, you don't think so, but there might have been perhaps."

"No. No, I'm sure there weren't. Of course Mr. Dearden phoned his brother-in-law as soon as we got back into the house after—after seeing what had happened. And he heard then about his sister's accident and why it was that his father had come home."

"But you don't remember any incoming calls?"

"No."

"What time was it when you got here from the station?"

"I think it was about twelve."

"And Mrs. Haslam's accident, I understand from what Mr. Dearden has just told me, happened about then too. So Sir Lucas could hardly have made up his mind to come home until a little later. So if he or anyone else had phoned to say he was coming, it would have been later than midday."

"Of course."

"And you'd have heard the telephone, if it had rung, or do you think you might not have done so?"

"Certainly I should have, and no one rang," she said. "Mr. and Mrs. Dearden had no way of knowing that Sir Lucas was expected home, and so could not have planted a bomb in the lane to murder him, if that's what you're insinuating."

"Just covering a small point," he said. "I'm sorry, it's my job. Nothing important."

THREE

"AND YOU DON'T WANT ME HERE," Dorothea said. "It's all right if I go next door."

"Perfectly, perfectly. We'll be leaving ourselves." Roland stood up. "We'll be in touch," he said, a remark which Andrew found ominous.

The detectives waited until after Dorothea and Lyn had left, then followed towards the door. But just before leaving, Roland turned once more to Colin.

"Waterman, you said."

"Yes," Colin answered.

"You're certain of that?"

"It's what the landlord at the pub told me. I don't know it of my own knowledge, if that's the right way of putting it."

"Interesting, all the same. I think we'll call at The Running Man."

"Is it true that a man called Waterman committed a murder and that Sir Lucas was the prosecuting counsel?" Colin asked.

"Could be. Have to check it up, of course. But it could be. Useful information, anyway. Thank you."

Roland and Sergeant Porter went out into the night, which had become quite dark now that even the last flickering of the flames in the lane had been extinguished.

As the front door closed behind them, Jonathan helped himself to more sherry. Sitting down near to the fire, he observed, "There's something they'll be asking about soon besides that telephone call that didn't happen." He looked at Andrew. "You've thought of it already, I expect. I've a feeling it's the sort of thing you would think of."

"If you mean, where did the explosive device, as they called it, come from . . ." Andrew paused.

Jonathan nodded with a slight smile on his face. It was a sardonic smile which suddenly made his face look much older than it had a moment before.

"That's it, of course," he said. "And you realise, I'm an excellent suspect. I work for a big construction firm, and at the moment you could also call them a destruction firm, because they happen to have been blowing up a block of flats built in the fifties, which has turned out to be a death-trap. So I could quite easily have laid my hands on some explosive. I wonder if it would be sensible of me to point that out to the police myself, or wait for them to find it out."

"For God's sake, this isn't a joke!" Colin said harshly.

"I wasn't joking," Jonathan replied.

"Then you'd better not speak till you're spoken to!"

It was an injunction that Andrew had not heard since his childhood, and even then his parents, having been very reasonable people, had never meant it seriously.

"If Waterman is the man you think he is," he said to Colin, "he may have made many useful connections in the bomb business while he was in prison."

"But how did he know Lucas was coming here?" Colin asked. "That's the question we always have to come back to."

"Yes, how he was coming and when," Andrew said. "But I

believe the Watermans of this earth have all sorts of ways of obtaining and spreading information."

"Well, don't start chatting to the police about explosives, Jonathan," Colin said, "at least until you've thought of a motive for yourself. They won't really be interested in you till you come up with a good motive for killing poor Lucas. If you want to feel important, I'd concentrate on that."

"Oh, if I wanted to feel important I could do better than that." Jonathan spoke with a cheerfulness that seemed to Andrew not quite suitable to the occasion, yet suddenly remembering Jonathan as a child, it occurred to him that it had always been there—a lively awareness of what was going on around him rather than depression during unexpected troubles. Andrew looked at him with more interest than he had felt before.

"Of course, that man Waterman has the most obvious motive," Jonathan went on, "though there's that problem of how he knew Lucas would be coming home when he did. Then there are other people we know nothing about, I mean people like Waterman who've somehow been harmed by Lucas and who wanted revenge. Perhaps, it isn't impossible, Lucas got in touch with someone when he was in London without Henry knowing anything about it, and that person knew approximately when Lucas might be expected here. Then there's Henry himself."

His father gave him a thoughtful look, as if he were trying to make up his mind whether or not to take him seriously, then shook his head.

"I wish you wouldn't talk nonsense," he said. "What d'you mean by saying there's Henry himself?"

"I don't really know," Jonathan said, "except that he's the one person who definitely knew that Lucas was coming home."

"But he was in London, we know that for sure, because he was there when Nicholas telephoned." But Colin's tone was less confident than before. "I suppose the police could be wrong and the bomb could have been planted in the car in London and not here in the lane, and it was just something going wrong with the timing device that stopped it going off till Lucas was nearly home. But what possible motive could Henry have had for murdering his father-in-law? I think he was the richer of the two, and so far as I know had never had any quarrel with him."

"May I ask something?" Andrew said. "Just what does Henry do? How has it come about that he's richer than Sir Lucas, who must have been pretty well fixed?"

"Henry's a senior partner in a notable firm of accountants," Colin answered. "The sort of people who do jobs for the government and that kind of thing. Oh, Henry isn't short of money. He can't be if he can afford to leave his wife in St. Raphael's."

"So whom else have you in mind?" Andrew asked Jonathan, genuinely curious about what the young man would say.

Jonathan seemed to take a kind of pleasure in being consulted.

"Oh, of course there's Nicholas," he said. "If I'd been Nicholas I've have got around to murdering the old man long ago."

"I do wish you wouldn't be flippant," Colin said. "There's nothing funny about what's happened this evening."

"But I'm not being flippant," Jonathan assured him. "Nicholas has the best of all motives for killing Lucas. Money and hatred."

"Hatred?" Andrew said.

"Oh yes, lots of hatred seething under that gentle surface of his," Jonathan said. "His father was a spectacularly successful man, wasn't he? And Nicholas hasn't done too badly in his own line, but he's never in his life written anything near a best seller. I suppose he earns enough to keep himself and Gwen without being actually dependent on the old man, but if they didn't live in that rather fine old house and do a

good deal of looking after him and making his life comfortable, they'd be much nearer to the bread line. By which I
only mean a semi-detached in some London suburb, with a
cleaning woman perhaps once a week and some kind of not
very impressive second-hand car. And I wouldn't put it past
Lucas to have rubbed that in. But I'm sure when his will's
read it'll turn out he's left his money equally between Nicholas and Erica, which will be very nice for both of them."

"All right, so we know Nicholas had a possible motive for
murdering his father," Colin said, "but how did he know
Erica was going to be in a car smash this morning? How did
he know his father would be coming home this evening? It
always comes back to that. If Lyn's right that there were no
telephone calls today, how could he possibly have known
when and where to plant the bomb?"

"Another question," Andrew said. "When did he get hold
of it, or construct it? It isn't a thing you can toss off in a few
minutes."

"Oh God, I suppose I'm not being really serious after all,"
Jonathan answered. "I mean, I don't seriously think Nicholas
would have murdered his father. But a possible way he could
have got hold of a bomb—no, I don't think it's really a possibility—all the same, last summer Nicholas and Gwen went
off to Spain by car, and I've an idea he may have had some
connection with some rather shady characters there, Basque
separatists and so on. He's fond of doing what he calls research for those spy stories of his, and so . . . No, I'm talking absolute nonsense. Don't take any notice of it."

"And what about Gwen?" Colin asked. "Has she any motive?"

"The same as Nicholas's, I suppose," Jonathan said. "She
may have got very bored looking after the old man, most of
the burden of which, I imagine, used to fall on her, and she
may have thought it would be nice to inherit his money. But
I can't see her planting a bomb, even if she and Nicholas
managed to get hold of one in Spain. And she doesn't seem to

have had any more knowledge than he had about Lucas coming home. That's to say, if it's true that there were no telephone calls from London after Erica's accident."

"That young woman, Lyn Goddard, who said there weren't," Andrew said, "who is she exactly? What's her connection with the Deardens? What does she do? Why is she here? You seem to know her."

"I think her connection with the Deardens is simply that she's an old school friend of Gwen's, or something of that sort," Jonathan said. "Anyway, she's been coming and going to that house for as long as we've lived here. What does she do? Well, I think she's something vaguely connected with the BBC, though I don't know exactly what. Something editorial, I think. And she's here of course for the same reason as you are, it's Christmas. I believe she was here for Christmas last year. I don't think she's any family of her own, and to the best of my belief she's never been married. She's never mentioned it that I can remember. If there've been men in her life, it wouldn't surprise me. She's attractive in her way, wouldn't you say? But I can't remember her ever talking about anyone special."

"And what was her relationship with Sir Lucas?" Andrew asked.

Jonathan gave him a startled look. He did not seem inclined to answer the question, and actually it was only at this reluctance that Andrew began to wonder if the question related to something more important than he had realised.

After a moment Jonathan remarked, "You ask the damndest questions, Andrew. I don't think she had any special relationship with Lucas. Though I wonder . . . No, it isn't possible."

"What do you mean?" his father asked irritably. "What isn't possible?"

Jonathan shook his head. "No, it was just a fantastic thought that came into my head when Andrew asked that fantastic question. What was her relationship with Lucas?

Was there ever anything between them, that's what he
wanted to know. After all, Lucas can't have been all that old
when she was first intimate with the family, and suppose he's
the reason she never settled down to living with any other
man. I know I'm talking like a fool. Andrew shouldn't have
got me started on it. But if there was a time a few years ago
when she thought she and Lucas were going to get married,
and if it happened she knew she'd been remembered in his
will, then the revenge motive because he'd got out of the
marriage, and then her hoping to benefit . . . I'm sorry, Andrew, you really shouldn't have started asking impossible
questions. She's a very nice girl. If you like, I'll think of a
motive why you might have murdered Lucas yourself."

"I can only think of one," Andrew said. "The fact is, I have
never committed a murder. But I have been involved, much
against my will, in helping the police with problems that
have arisen out of one or two. And yet I have never even
begun to understand the feelings of a murderer. Well, is this a
serious failure on my part? I am old, I am retired, I have been
engaged for years in writing a book which I shall probably
never finish, even though I have a contract for it, and I am
sure some misguided people think that I am a very wise old
man. Yet I am utterly at sea when I try to comprehend what
leads a person to the act of killing another. So if it would
enlarge my understanding of mankind before I die, I might
try to find out what it's really like. But I can assure you that
if I ever do commit a murder it would not be with a bomb.
For one thing, I intensely dislike loud noises. I find even the
friendliest of parties, where everyone by degrees talks louder
and louder in order to be heard at all, a fearful strain. And I
am not mechanically minded. Even if I had all the explosive
in the world on hand, I would not know how to construct a
bomb. And I suspect the same might be said of Miss Goddard. Can you really see her constructing a bomb in secret,
then carrying it around in her handbag, one doesn't know for
how long, until she found a suitable opportunity for blowing

up Sir Lucas? It's true I don't understand the young of the present day, but does it seem probable?"

Jonathan grinned at him.

"You didn't really need to convince us, you know," he said. "Nobody is going to think either you or Lyn are murderers."

"I'm afraid I may have sounded rather pompous," Andrew said.

"You did, just a bit," Jonathan said, "but we know that attitude is one of your many disguises. You're so afraid someone might start thinking you really are quite wise that you make it sound absurd on purpose. I wish I knew what you really think about what's happened."

"So do I," Andrew said. "So do I."

They heard the sound of the front door being opened and a moment later Dorothea came into the room. Somehow she looked even smaller than usual, shrunken and chilled. She went straight to Colin and put her arms round his neck, hiding her face against him. He held her in his arms, clasping her to him until she wanted to speak.

After a moment she raised her head. "You know, Gwen thinks Nicholas did it," she said. "Can you imagine it? Suddenly making up your mind your husband's a murderer?"

"It's shock," Colin said. "She'll have second thoughts tomorrow."

"You don't . . ." She paused, and still holding tightly to Colin, looked round the room. "You don't think she could be right?"

"Look, how long have we known Nicholas?" Colin asked. "Ten years, twelve years? Have you ever wondered if he could be capable of a peculiarly atrocious kind of murder?"

She did not answer at first, then shook her head.

"Has it ever occurred to you that I might be?" he said.

The quiet common sense in his tone seemed to have an effect on her.

"Don't be ridiculous," she said.

"But shock can do extraordinary things to people," he said.

"You know, by tomorrow she may have forgotten everything she said tonight."

"Suppose she hasn't," Jonathan said.

"I'd sooner not suppose anything of the kind," Colin said. "And I don't think it would be a bad idea if we all went to bed. We'll probably have the police here again tomorrow. I foresee a busy day."

He propelled Dorothea firmly out of the room and upstairs to their bedroom.

Jonathan lingered, looking at Andrew with the same smile that a short while before he had thought sardonic.

"I wonder what life is like if you haven't got such understanding parents as I have," Jonathan said. "I'm very lucky, I suppose."

"Don't you think so yourself?" Andrew asked.

"Oh yes. Yes, certainly. Sometimes I think too lucky."

"Why d'you think that?"

Jonathan stood up, stretching and yawning deeply.

"Of course I don't really. It just seems to me sometimes that life's been made almost too easy for me. When something appalling happens, I don't know how to behave. Would you say I'm normally mature for my age? I've never yet had to cope with any responsibility."

"Perhaps immaturity is one of your many disguises," Andrew said.

"Oh God, I might have known I wouldn't get a real answer from you. You're the most evasive man I ever met. Goodnight. Will you turn the lights out and so on?"

"Good-night," Andrew said as Jonathan went out of the room.

Andrew soon followed him, after switching off the electric fire and turning off the lights in the room, but it was some time before he went to bed. He had brought a Rex Stout with him, and after getting into his pyjamas and dressing-gown he settled down to read for a while before thinking of trying to sleep.

But what happened to him was that almost at once he fell asleep in his chair; when later he woke with a start, he found that it was nearly half past one—at least two hours later than his normal time for going to bed. His book had fallen to the floor and his mind was in a bemused state, actually uncertain for a few minutes of where he was and how he had managed to arrive in this pleasant but unfamiliar room.

Then, as memory of the evening came back to him, a feeling that there was something about it still eluding his memory began to disturb him. It was something to do with Lyn Goddard. He did his best to close his mind to it, got into bed and switched off the bedside lamp. But immediately the darkness of the room seemed to be lit by the lurid flames of the fire in the lane, a horror that he would never forget, and closing his eyes against it did not help.

He wondered if anyone else in the house was asleep. For a while he tossed and turned, only to find himself presently at King's Cross Station, attempting to travel he could not remember where. He had a ticket which should have told him where he intended to go, but it appeared to be written in a foreign language, possibly Chinese. He started asking people where they thought he ought to go, but they only looked at him superciliously and hurried on their way. He wandered about for a little, finding himself among strange buildings, totally lost and in a mood of frenzied frustration, while smoke filled the streets though there was no sign of anything being on fire. It was a great relief when he suddenly woke to find daylight at the window and Dorothea at his bedside with a breakfast tray in her hands.

"This is really very good of you," he said, "but you shouldn't have troubled."

"I'm sure you like breakfast in bed," she said, "and it's no trouble at all."

"Is it very late?" he asked. "Have I overslept very badly?"

"No, it's only eight o'clock," she answered. "And I've

given you that little bit of cheese with your breakfast, as well as the coffee and toast. That's right, isn't it?"

He raised himself against the pillows, giving a self-conscious smile.

"I'm sure it's only a superstition," he said, "and by now really only a habit, but for a time I was convinced that it did one good to start the day with some protein, and cheese seemed the easiest way to do that. I'm too lazy to boil myself an egg. But I think it's time I cured myself of it."

"Oh, I shouldn't do that," she said. "A little superstition is good for all of us, otherwise we become too intellectually austere. I believe in a lot of ridiculous things myself which I wouldn't dream of trying to justify to a scientist like you, but which somehow satisfy me. I hope you slept well."

"Excellently," Andrew replied untruthfully. As she left the room he started nibbling the small piece of Cheddar cheese that he found on the tray.

It was nearly ten o'clock when he came downstairs. He could hear the clicking of Colin's typewriter and Dorothea busy in the kitchen. There was no sign of Jonathan, who presumably had left long ago for work. It all seemed a little strangely normal. And the day happened to be December the twenty-fourth, Christmas Eve.

When Andrew was a child Christmas Eve had always been a day of great tension and expectation. In the evening the Christmas tree would be lit up, but it was what happened next day that counted. He had not been brought up to believe in Santa Claus and had never hung a stocking up in the sitting-room fireplace in the hope of gifts; but he had assumed nonetheless that when he came down to breakfast next morning there would be a splendid collection of presents for him, done up in colourful wrappings, around the base of the Christmas tree. The morning then could be happily spent unwrapping them until it was time to prepare himself for turkey and plum pudding.

Usually this would be followed by a very small glass of

port, his first taste of alcohol, which it happened that he heartily disliked, though he had pretended to enjoy it. And by then perhaps the thought would have inserted itself into his consciousness that, delightful as several of the presents were, he would be compelled during the next day or two to write letters of thanks to the people who had been so kind as to send them. This would be dreadfully hard work, even though the letters would always be the same. He would state that he hoped the recipient was very well, that he himself was very well, that his mother and father were very well, and that he was very grateful for the present he had just received and which happened to be just what he wanted, and that he was their affectionate grandchild, or nephew, or friend, as the case might be, Andrew. After that life would return to normal.

Sometimes the presents had really been what he had wanted, such as those that came yearly from the great-aunt who, in addition to providing cucumber sandwiches, had saved herself the trouble of trying to imagine what a young boy might really like by sending him a one-pound note, usually enclosed in a Christmas card depicting the Holy Family arriving in poverty at their stable. With the increase of inflation, or perhaps in recognition of his advancing years, the one pound had gradually risen to five, but his letters to the good old lady, perhaps increasing a little in warmth as he became more literate, had not substantially altered. She was of course long since dead, yet as he went into the Cahills' sitting-room and saw the sprays of holly stuck behind the picture frames, reaffirming to him that this was Christmas Eve, it occurred to him that his letters of thanks, which even now he occasionally had to write, were really no great advance on what he had written long ago.

He had sat down by the fire and was looking with an interest that he did not quite understand at Dorothea's improvised Christmas tree, hung with Christmas cards, when the doorbell rang and he heard Dorothea go to answer it. In a moment she came into the sitting-room bringing Detective Chief Inspector Roland and Detective Sergeant Porter with her. Andrew rose to greet them and she assured them hurriedly that she would fetch her husband.

The inspector said, "I'm not sure if that's necessary, Mrs. Cahill. It's Professor Basnett we really want a word with."

"But I'll fetch my husband," she said, and went scuttling out of the room. Andrew heard her running up the stairs, and a moment later the sound of Colin's typewriter ceased.

"Nice day," Roland said, accepting Andrew's invitation that he should be seated. "Surprisingly warm for the time of year. But it was on the news last night that there's a depression on its way."

Andrew had not yet taken in anything about the weather, but looking out of a window now he saw a patch of blue sky, bordered by bustling clouds; there was enough wind to make the leafless beeches at the edge of the garden bend and sway a little.

"A depression? Well, of course they could be wrong," he said.

"Have you ever wondered what it feels like to be a weatherman?" Roland asked. "I mean, to speak with all that authority and all those diagrams to back you up, and then at least fifty percent of the time being wrong."

"Fifty percent?" Andrew said. "Is it really as often as that?"

"Well, I couldn't swear to it, but that's how it feels. If I was wrong as often in my job—but then, perhaps I am. I'd be the last person to know, wouldn't I?" Then, the ice between the two Englishmen having been broken by some remarks about the weather, he turned to the sergeant who was carrying a briefcase and said, "Bob, the photographs."

Sergeant Porter opened the briefcase, extracted a large envelope and handed it to the inspector. He drew a photograph out of it and handed it to Andrew.

"Mean anything to you?" he asked.

Andrew looked at the long face with its long, thin nose, the almost lipless mouth and the small eyes that were not quite on the same level.

"It's the man who came here yesterday morning, asking for Sir Lucas," he said. "That's what you wanted to know, isn't it?"

"Sure of that?"

"Absolutely." Andrew handed the photograph back to Roland, who slid it into its envelope and returned it to Porter. "Is he Thomas Waterman?"

"That's right," Roland said. "A man who got life for murdering his wife and did about eight years in prison. He came out about three months ago."

"Is it true that Sir Lucas was the prosecuting counsel who got him convicted?" Andrew asked.

"Yes, that's true. And Waterman threatened him and the judge from the dock. But that doesn't mean anything. A good many people do that, but have time to forget all about it during the years of their sentence."

"What were the circumstances of the murder?"

Roland gave a slight shrug. "Jealousy, well justified. The woman was a tart who used to bring her customers into their home when her husband was at work. Then he came home unexpectedly and caught her with the current client, who gave Waterman a beating before bolting. And Waterman fell on his wife and beat her to death. It was doubtful if he even knew what he was doing. The circumstances were why the sentence wasn't more severe. Anyway, as I remember the case and what I've been able to dig up about him since last night, he was always a pretty unstable character. He made a very bad impression on the jury by a mixture of arrogance and dead silence until he shouted his threats. But there's something I particularly want to ask you, Professor. Did you give Waterman any suggestion, even the faintest hint, that Sir Lucas was expected home in the afternoon?"

Andrew shook his head. "I couldn't have, because I didn't know it myself. I did say Sir Lucas was in London."

"And you didn't add anything, even by accident, which Waterman could have construed as meaning that he was coming home?"

"I'm quite certain I didn't."

"I see. Thanks."

The inspector stood up and seemed ready to leave the room when Colin and Dorothea came hurrying in. Roland hesitated for a moment, then reached out his hand to the sergeant for the photograph. He handed it to Colin.

"Have you ever seen that man anywhere?" he asked.

Colin looked at it thoughtfully. "No," he said. "No, I'm quite sure . . . Yes, I *am* sure, and yet there's a certain familiarity . . . No, I don't mean that. I'm sure I've never seen him. Who is it?"

"A man called Thomas Waterman."

"Who's staying at The Running Man? But I didn't see him there."

Dorothea had taken the photograph from Colin.

"I know what it is," she said. "You're remembering photographs of him in the newspapers at the time of his trial."

"Yes, that must be it, though it's so long ago," Colin said to Roland. "It's a very long time ago, isn't it?"

"Longish." Roland took the photograph and handed it back to Porter.

"But hasn't anybody seen him here?" Colin asked. "I mean, besides Professor Basnett?"

"Yes, several people. The fact is, he's still at The Running Man. He's under observation. Probably we'll have to take him in for questioning. Well, we mustn't keep you. Thank you for your help."

The two detectives were just about to leave when the doorbell rang again.

This time it was Nicholas. With his hair combed and his face recently shaved, he looked neat in his corduroy trousers and cardigan, but he had the appearance of someone who had not had much sleep the night before. His eyes were hollow, his cheeks sagged. His shaggy eyebrows twitched into a frown when he saw the two policemen.

"I'm sorry, am I interrupting anything?" he asked. "I can come back later."

"Not at all. We were just leaving," Roland said. "In fact we were coming round to see you. Perhaps you could save us some trouble."

He held out his hand to the sergeant, who once more handed him the envelope with the photograph in it. Roland took the photograph and showed it to Nicholas.

"Have you ever seen this man?" Roland asked.

Nicholas's eyebrows lifted suddenly as if he had just received a shock. He went on looking at it without saying anything.

"You have seen him," Roland said.

"Not for a very long time," Nicholas answered. "It's Waterman, isn't it?"

"So you know him," Roland said.

"Not exactly. I remember his name, of course, from the time of the murder. But I can't have met him more than once or twice, and that only very briefly."

"How did that happen?"

Dorothea suddenly interrupted to beg them all to sit down, and asked if they would like coffee. The coffee was refused, but all of them except Andrew sat down. Andrew went to a window and stood looking out at the garden, which still had brown leaves from the beeches scattered across the lawn. Some winter jasmine was in bloom, its delicate, fresh-looking yellow flowers seeming strangely gone astray in the wintry scene.

For some reason he had started to think about the dream that he had had in the night, and how in it he had gone wandering, lost along smoke-filled streets where there was no fire to be seen, and how that had been peculiarly frightening.

There had been a fierce fire in the lane the night before and that no doubt had been why in his dream, with memories in his conscious mind of the fire in the King's Cross Underground, he had found himself at King's Cross Station, trying to read a ticket written in an unintelligible script. But why should he be thinking of it now? Normally he never remembered his dreams for more than a few minutes after waking.

"He was a clerk in my brother-in-law's office," Nicholas said. "Not that Henry was my brother-in-law at the time. He and my sister weren't even engaged. If they had been I don't suppose my father could have taken the case. I mean, if there had been even a fairly remote family connection it wouldn't have been ethical for him to do it. In those days Henry Haslam was my accountant and a not very intimate friend. I don't think he and my sister even met till two or three years later. But I did call in on him in his office two or three times, and I remembered that clerk when his photograph started appearing in the papers, mostly because of his strange eyes and the thin, bitter face, the air of suspiciousness and a sort of contained anger. Or perhaps that's just what I thought when I knew about his crime. It's very difficult to be sure of a thing like that after such a long time."

"But you're sure he had a connection with your brother-in-law, are you?" Roland said.

"Oh yes, I'm sure of that," Nicholas answered. "We discussed it all once or twice, though on the whole he seemed rather naturally to prefer not to talk about it."

"And it happens that Mr. Haslam is the one person we know of who definitely knew Sir Lucas was coming home yesterday afternoon."

"Yes, but . . . You don't mean you think there's still some connection between them."

"Perhaps not. But it's the sort of possibility one has to take into consideration."

"I don't understand," Nicholas said. "Henry was in London yesterday. He couldn't have planted the bomb. That's certain. And . . . Oh, I see! You think he somehow got in touch with Waterman and Waterman planted it for him. That's ludicrous."

"I daresay it is. But I come back to the fact that Mr. Haslam knew Sir Lucas was on his way home."

"Yes, that's quite true," Nicholas agreed. "I've been talking to him on the telephone this morning and he pointed out himself that he seemed to be the only person who knew of my father's change of plan. But apart from the fact that I can't see him getting in touch with Waterman to arrange that explosion for him, he'd nothing whatever to gain by my father's death. He's a wealthy man himself. He doesn't need money. And to the best of my knowledge he and my father liked each other. I think they were good friends."

"Suppose we turn things round the other way," Roland said. "Suppose it was Waterman who got in touch with Mr. Haslam. Suppose—this is just a suggestion—Waterman has some kind of hold over Mr. Haslam. As a clerk in his office he might possibly be a fairly skilled accountant himself. Suppose at some time he'd spotted some irregularity, possibly simply some mistake, in the work of the firm and managed to keep a record of it over all these years. And suppose when he heard from Professor Basnett that Sir Lucas was in London, mightn't he have deduced that he'd be staying, or at least spending some of his time with his daughter and son-in-law, and demanded information about his probable movements? It might not have occurred to Waterman at that stage of things that Sir Lucas would actually be coming home and so be vulnerable here. He might have planned to go to London and somehow track Sir Lucas down there."

Andrew had turned and was watching the two men with interest. Roland's thick eyelids were lifted higher than usual, and his eyes were concentrated intently on Nicholas's tired face, which looked blank with incredulity.

"You don't know my brother-in-law!" he exclaimed. "Waterman have some hold on him for misdoings in his past!

Henry is the most upright man who ever lived. He's a pillar of righteousness. No, if Waterman did get in touch with him, it's possible Henry might have given him a helping hand out of compassion, and I suppose it's just conceivable he might accidentally have let slip that my father was on his way home, but I'd be surprised if he'd have done even that. He'd have remembered that my father had prosecuted Waterman and that Waterman, long ago as it was, might not have forgotten the threat he shouted from the dock. No, if you pursue that line, Inspector, I'm sure you'll only be wasting your time."

"I see. Thank you." Roland stood up once more. "I'm very grateful to you for this discussion. It's very useful to have explored these odd ideas of mine even if they don't seem important. That's beautiful holly you've got for your decorations, Mrs. Cahill. All we've got at home are plastic, not at all the same thing. Good morning."

Colin saw him and the sergeant to the door.

Nicholas let out a deep breath, as if he were relieved at their going.

"Now what did he mean by that?" he asked, as he appeared to relax.

"That real holly's nicer than plastic holly?" Dorothea said. "Well, of course it is."

"No, that our talk has been useful," Nicholas said. "All I did was tell him that his ideas were no good."

"That may have been very useful," Andrew said. "When you want to tidy up your thoughts, the first thing to do is to get the useless rubbish out of the way."

"You think that's all it was? I didn't say something . . . ?" Nicholas paused, then shook his head. "No, I didn't. How could I? But I ought to tell you why I really came over this morning. It was just to ask you if you'll forgive us if we call that Christmas dinner off. It's a pity. We were really looking forward to it. But Gwen isn't in a state to cope. I expect you can understand that."

"Of course," Dorothea said. "We weren't expecting it to go ahead. Please tell her not to worry about it."

"I'll bring you the turkey as a present, if you like," Nicholas said with a sad smile. "I expect we'll be having something out of the freezer."

"Put the turkey in the freezer too," she said, "and have it when the first of the shock's worn off. Of course it'll spoil it, but you can't help that. It may have spent a good deal of its life in a freezer already, or do I mean its death? Oh dear, I ought not to have said that, I mean, this isn't a time to be flippant about death, even a poor turkey's. Nicholas, we're all of us really terribly sorry for you and Gwen. I suppose you haven't got around to thinking of what you'll probably do. I mean, will you stay on in that house, or move away? We'd hate to have new neighbours."

"You might find them better value than us," Nicholas said. "But we haven't started to think about the future. The funny thing is, Gwen started talking of moving away only a little while ago. My father wasn't the easiest of men in the world to live with, and he was getting more difficult as he got older. Gwen got the worst of it and wanted to leave. She sometimes talked of going abroad. Yet now that my father's been killed I get the impression that she's been hit even harder than I'd have expected. I suppose it's more because of the horrible circumstances than out of grief. And besides that . . ." He stopped again.

"It's just shock, isn't it?" Dorothea said. "She doesn't actually believe you planted the bomb."

He gave her an astonished look. "What made you think of that?"

"It was just the way she was talking when I went over to see her yesterday evening," Dorothea said. "She seemed to have become frightened of you."

"Yes. Well, I know what you mean. No, I don't think she meant it, or anyway the fear's worn off by now. It was upsetting while it lasted, of course. It made everything feel just that little bit worse than it was already. But you know how—well, how highly strung she is. I didn't really take it very seriously. She does tend to dramatize things."

"I'd have thought you'd had enough drama yesterday without that," Colin said.

"I suppose it's possible she was feeling guilty because of the sort of things she's been saying about my father recently," Nicholas replied. "Perhaps she's really been hoping something would happen to him. Of course we're going to benefit a good deal financially and that rather increases one's sense of guilt. That house, for instance. As I said, we haven't started thinking about the future, but I suppose the fact is we shall sell it. I believe the way my father left his money is half and half between Erica and me, and if that's so the place will have to be valued—it must be worth an enormous amount these days—and keeping it might eat up a big part of our share, so it'll be simplest to sell it and split the proceeds with Erica. But I just don't know." He stood up. "You really think I convinced that detective with what I said about Henry? I didn't say anything he could have misunderstood?"

"I'm sure you couldn't have," Colin said. "You told him Henry had admitted he knew Lucas was coming home and also that he knew Waterman, who couldn't possibly have had any hold over him, as Henry was what I think you called a pillar of righteousness. And I think that was about all."

"Good, good." Nicholas made for the door and Colin saw him out.

FOUR

WHEN COLIN RETURNED there was a brief silence, then Dorothea disappeared to the kitchen to put together something for lunch. It turned out to be ham sandwiches and coffee. Afterwards Andrew felt his usual inclination to have a short nap, but Dorothea said that she was going into Rockford and wondered if Andrew would like to come with her for the drive.

"As we aren't having Christmas dinner with the Deardens, I'd better get something for us," she said. "I think a piece of sirloin, and perhaps some Côte du Rhone. I know the supermarket stocks that. Of course, none of us feels exactly like celebrating, but I don't see why we shouldn't have a good meal. I mean, even if it wasn't Christmas, there'd be nothing against that, would there? In fact it might somehow be easier if it wasn't Christmas, but of course we shan't feel that we're celebrating anything, we're just going ahead normally, though we can have some of my mince pies. Or do you feel there'd be something sacrilegious about eating mince pies in the circumstances? I simply couldn't bear just to throw them away. No, we'll have roast beef and mince pies. I think that will be quite suitable. Will you come with me, Andrew, or would you sooner have a little sleep?"

"I'd love to come with you," he said almost sincerely.

About two o'clock they set out together.

Rockford had once been a medium-sized market town, and it still had a centre of a market-place, old houses, old inns and a church. There were several shops that had once been what people called really good old family businesses, but which in the last few years had gradually been taken over by chain stores; this had changed their character, occasionally to their advantage. Also the town had spread in all directions, and now had—besides acres of council houses, costly bungalows and high-rise flats—a university of its own, some factories and offices of a number of national and even international companies; it was in one of these, Brown, Bretherton, that Jonathan worked.

Parking, as it would have been in all towns of the Rockford type, was the problem most on Dorothea's mind as she and Andrew drove into it in her Ford Escort. But she was fortunate in the main city car-park to be able to swerve sharply into a space left empty just before she reached it by someone else driving out. Someone in the car ahead of her, who might have been said to have more right to the space than she had, shouted something at her which was angry and probably obscene, but she was untroubled by it. With her shopping-basket over her arm, she and Andrew set off towards one of the supermarkets at the town's centre.

She found all that she wanted fairly easily, then thought of a number of other things which she might as well buy since she was on the spot, and the basket, which Andrew had taken from her, grew heavier. Then they started back towards the car-park, but they were only just outside the door of the store when she suddenly suggested that perhaps they might have a cup of tea.

"There's a little place only just along here," she said. "How do you feel about it?"

Andrew did not feel at all like a cup of tea, but as it was evident that she wanted one—whether for the sake of the tea or because, as he rather suspected, she wanted a chance to talk to him quietly where there would not be even Colin to overhear them—he said that it seemed an excellent idea. They made their way along the pavement, busy with the crowds of people who were doing their last-minute Christmas shopping, to a small café between two office blocks where there were small round tables with plastic tops, a self-service counter and a great many brightly coloured paper streamers pinned along the walls to celebrate the season. Dorothea firmly planted Andrew at one of the tables with the basket of shopping, and went off to the counter to collect their cups of tea.

That it was to talk with him rather than to drink the very pale brown liquid with which she returned was evident almost as soon as she sat down.

"Andrew, what do you think of Jonathan?" she asked.

It was said with an earnestness that suggested she wanted more than a casual answer. But the only one that he could think of for the moment was, "He seems a very nice lad."

"Yes, yes, of course, but do you think—?" She took some time to decide how to frame her next sentence. "Is he happy?"

"You know I hardly know him," he said. "The fact that Nell and I occasionally spent a summer holiday by the sea with you when he was about ten years old doesn't mean I know much about him now."

"I'm not sure that it doesn't," she said. "It lays a foundation of trust." She stirred her tea vigorously with her spoon, although she had put no sugar in it. "I'm not trying to get you to tell me anything that he's told you in confidence. I wouldn't think of doing that."

"He hasn't told me anything in confidence," Andrew said. "Truly, not a thing."

She gave a sigh. "He seems so frank and open, doesn't he? Yet these days he never really tells me anything about himself."

"Perhaps there isn't much to tell," he suggested. "Perhaps he really is what he seems."

"And you think he's happy?"

"Honestly I haven't thought about it," he said. "It's one of the hardest things to gauge unless a person decides to tell you about it. The happiest people on earth may have terrible lines on their faces, and the unhappiest may look bland and pink. Anyway, why do you think he isn't? That's what interests me at the moment."

"Oh, I don't know. Well, no, perhaps I do. Oh, I don't know."

He waited silently for her to go on.

"I could be so wrong," she said at length, "and that makes it stupid even to try to talk about it. I mean, the present-day young are so different from what even Colin and I were like when we were young, and for someone of your age, I don't mean to say you're old, but all the same I should say they're an utter mystery."

"I don't deny that I'm old," Andrew said, "and I don't deny the young sometimes puzzle me, but they puzzled me even when I was young myself. Other people have always puzzled me. But how dull life would be if they didn't. An open book, with the pages hardly worth turning. But what's really worrying you about Jonathan, Dorothea?"

"I think he's in love with Gwen," she said.

"Oh," he said. "Oh, I see."

"I wonder if you do," she said. "The fact is, it's only a feeling I've got. He's never said anything. I haven't any evidence that there's anything in this idea of mine at all. But there's something about the way he looks at her when we're all together, and then the fact which probably doesn't mean anything that they go off for long walks together— Oh, don't I sound horrible, like a suspicious sort of Victorian mamma? But really I'm not. It's just that I so terribly don't want him to get badly hurt."

"Does Colin think the same as you?" Andrew asked.

"I don't know. We've never discussed it."

"That surprises me," he said. "I had a sort of impression that you and he discuss nearly everything."

"So we do."

"But not this particular worry of yours."

"No. You see, Colin can be so full of common sense, and when I have some really fantastic idea in my head, which I sometimes have, I tend rather to keep it to myself in case he pours cold water over it. But just now I feel I've simply got to talk about it to someone."

"And you think I can stand up to a bit of fantasy."

"Does that annoy you?"

"Of course not. But tell me, what about Gwen? Do you think she reciprocates this feeling Jonathan may have for her? If what Nicholas told us is true, that she wants to go and live abroad, it doesn't really sound like it."

"I haven't the faintest idea. But it isn't improbable, is it, that she's taken to him? He's very attractive, wouldn't you say? Or is that just maternal prejudice? And they do go off for long walks together and I've an idea Nicholas doesn't much like it, though it's true that sometimes, if Gwen doesn't feel like it for some reason, he goes instead of her and Jonathan never shows any sign that that's a disappointment. But he wouldn't, would he? I mean, if this is something that he and Gwen are keeping secret, he'd do his best to hide his real feelings."

"You know, I think there's something about all this that you aren't telling me, Dorothea," he said. "What is it?"

She drew a deep breath, seemed about to speak, then stopped herself and drank a little tea. Andrew looked at his and wondered if it would hurt her feelings if he left his undrunk. But then he nerved himself to pick up his cup, and drank about half of what was in it all at once.

"It's all because of the bomb, isn't it?" he said. "You think Jonathan was the intended victim."

She gave a little shiver, then met his eyes with a look imploring understanding.

"Well, don't you think he may have been?" she said.

"The thought of course had crossed my mind," Andrew said. "No one appears to have known that Dearden was expected home, but a lot of people knew that Jonathan would be driving along the lane only a few minutes before the time when the bomb went off. And the only person you can think of at the moment who might have had a motive for murdering Jonathan is Nicholas, if he believed there was something between Jonathan and Gwen."

"And don't you see, if there's anything in all this," she said, speaking rapidly, "he's still in frightful danger? If Nicholas is capable of doing something so frightful and failed, he won't leave it at that, he'll try again."

"But do you honestly think he's capable of such a thing?"

"Why not?"

Andrew picked up his cup again and this time succeeded in emptying it.

"You're one of the people who believe we're all capable of murder," he said.

"I'm not saying we all are," she said. "I'm only saying Nicholas might be."

"Of course you know him better than I do, but it isn't how he struck me."

"So you don't think there's anything in what I've been saying?"

He felt that in another moment he might be accused of having too much common sense.

"Let's say I'm not entirely convinced," he said. "This belief of yours that Jonathan and Gwen may be in love with one another—would they really need in these days to keep it so heavily concealed? There are several things they could do about it."

"Such as?"

"They could tell Nicholas about it, she could leave him, be divorced and marry Jonathan. Or if they couldn't bother with a divorce they could simply go away and live together. Or if she doesn't really care as much for Jonathan as he does for her, she could go on living happily with Nicholas and keeping Jonathan on a string, which might even be a help to Nicholas as he wouldn't have to bother about her being bored while he gets ahead with his writing. That last idea rather appeals to me."

"I suppose it would account for the way Jonathan has insisted on going on living with us," she said broodingly, appearing to take the suggestion seriously. "He and Gwen can see each other as often as they like without having to get in too deep. But you really think I've been talking nonsense, don't you, Andrew?"

"No, I just think it may be like one of the things which the good inspector thought it was useful to talk about."

"Rubbish, you mean, to be cleared out of the way."

"Something like that."

"And you honestly think Jonathan isn't in any danger?"

Andrew suddenly found himself very unwilling to respond. To be wrong in such a matter might be almost a kind of guilt.

"Forgetting Nicholas for the moment," he said, "has Jonathan any other enemies?"

"How can I know that? He wouldn't tell me." For a moment it looked as if she might burst into tears. But she controlled them, taking a few more cautious sips of her tea, then pushed her cup away. "If Jonathan wasn't the intended victim," she said, "if Lucas was really the target, we're back to the old question, aren't we—how did anyone know he'd be coming along the lane when he was? And I've had a thought about that. I know Lyn Goddard said that nobody phoned the Deardens yesterday, but suppose Inspector Roland's idea was more or less right and one of them phoned Henry and got the information from him then. She wouldn't have heard the telephone ringing, would she, if the telephoning was done from this end?"

"You're thinking of what Roland suggested about that man Waterman," Andrew said. "That he or someone telephoned Henry and so knew pretty precisely when Dearden would be coming along the lane. And if it was Waterman, he might not have known that Jonathan would be coming along it too and that he might even have come first and been the one to explode the bomb. But you're really thinking again of Nicholas, aren't you? He's your favourite suspect, whether his motive was to murder his wife's lover or to inherit his father's money. What have you really got against him, Dorothea?"

"Nothing," she said quickly. "Nothing at all. I like him."

"You're the best of friends, are you? Well, I hope the people who I think are my best friends don't nourish the sort of secret thoughts about me that you do about Nicholas."

She gave an uncertain laugh. "The funny thing is, I feel better for having talked to you like this, even if it's all nonsense. Thank you for listening, Andrew."

"And what's the next step? Do you tell any of this to the police?"

"The next step is we go home and have a drink. Then we'll finish the cold chicken and have some of that frozen lemon cream pie which you may have noticed me buying this afternoon. It'll have thawed by the time we get home. And I wouldn't dream of saying a word about all this to the police, or even to Colin either. Well, I'm not quite sure about that. I sometimes find myself meaning to keep something from him so as not to worry him, and then suddenly there I am, spilling it all. But you won't say anything about it yourself, will you?"

"You have my promise."

"And let's hope we have a nice quiet evening."

As it turned out, the evening was quiet enough, though not quite in the sense that Andrew thought Dorothea had intended. There were no sounds of bombs. There was no wailing of the sirens of police cars or ambulances, and as Jonathan had predicted, there were no carol singers. However, the doorbell rang more than once. The first time it was two very young and eager men, one of whom had a camera, who came from a Rockford newspaper and wanted to question the Cahills about the murder. Colin dealt with them, telling them that it was to the house next door that they should have gone. They said that they had been there already and had been advised to come here. He was gentle with them, partly because of their youth and inexperience, and partly because his own work was on the fringe of journalism, but he would not allow them into the house.

They took his photograph and some notes of what he said, and departed. But other representatives of the press who came later were not so easily got rid of, being aware that the story of the bomb in the lane would grow in importance. The Cahills and the Deardens played patball with them, each insisting that it was really the house next door that they wanted.

The sherry had been drunk and the chicken and the lemon cream pie had been eaten when the bell rang yet once more. The Cahills and Andrew were drinking coffee in the sitting-room.

Jonathan said, "For God's sake, don't answer it. We've had enough for one evening and probably it'll be worse tomorrow, when the news will have spread around. I shouldn't be surprised if there's something about it on television this evening."

The bell rang again.

"Go on, Jonathan, we'd better do something about it and I think it's your turn by now," Colin said. "You open it."

"But we've nothing to tell them," Jonathan grumbled.

"Never mind. Go on. There's no point in antagonising them."

Jonathan went out to the front door and a moment later returned, bringing in Lyn Goddard.

She was carrying a parcel roughly wrapped in brown paper. She was in the same grey dress as the day before, wore the same necklace and had the same air of composure which it seemed even a bomb could not shatter. Andrew wondered how real this composure was; whether perhaps she was one of the people who feel it an absolute necessity to conceal their feelings, having perhaps at some time encountered mockery or humiliation when they had failed to do so, but who then pay for this heavily in private. She certainly looked pale and tired, but as she held out the parcel that she was carrying to Colin her hands were steady, and when she spoke there was no sound of emotion in her soft, deep voice.

"Would you take a look at this?" she said. "Nicholas would like to know what you think of it."

Colin undid the brown paper wrapping. Inside was a bundle of papers, closely covered in handwriting. He riffled through them, then looked at Lyn.

"It's Lucas's memoirs," he said.

"It's the original manuscript," she said. "When he finished it he had it typed professionally, and it's the typed copy that went off to his agent. Nicholas's agent, of course, who agreed to do what he could for Lucas because of his connection with Nicholas. But Lucas kept this in his desk at home. Nicholas has read it, but he'd be grateful if you would too and tell him if you think it's important in any way. You'll see there are some things Lucas wrote in the first version which he crossed out before having it typed, but they're still quite easy to read. I haven't read it myself, so I can't have any opinions about it, but Nicholas says there are a few references to Waterman, which perhaps may mean something."

Colin looked at Andrew. "How would you like to tackle

the job first?" he asked. "Then Dorothea and I can read it
later and we can all discuss it."

"You don't mind doing it?" Lyn said to him.

"Of course not, if there's a chance it might help," Andrew
answered. "Does Nicholas really think there's something significant in it?"

"I don't know," she said. "I think he was being rather careful not to express an opinion in case I said anything that
might influence you. Anyway, I know he'll be very grateful
if you'll go through the thing."

"Sit down and have some coffee," Dorothea said. "I do
hope they're managing to feed you properly over there. If it
would make things easier for them and for you, you could
come over here and stay with us, or at least have your meals
with us. Gwen does seem rather to go to pieces in a crisis."

Lyn smiled faintly, as if she found the word "crisis" a
somewhat inadequate one for what had happened.

"She's always been like that, as long as I've known her,"
she said, "and that's since we were at school together. She
could get quite unbalanced at the mere thought of an exam in
the near future, then she'd do very well in it, while I, who
hadn't worried at all, came out somewhere near the bottom.
But she'll recover quite quickly, you'll find. Meanwhile I'm
doing most of the cooking and we shan't starve, though it's
very kind of you to invite me . . . No, thank you," she
added as Dorothea repeated her offer of coffee, "I'd better get
back."

She left, leaving Andrew with the same irritated feeling he
had had before that there was something he should have
asked her while he had the opportunity; but he still could not
remember what it was.

It was a slightly frightening feeling, this inefficiency of his
memory. He was not sure if it really was getting worse with
advancing age, or if it was merely something of which he had
recently become aware. Had he always been an example of
that stock joke, akin to the one about mothers-in-law—the

absent-minded professor? Whatever the truth about that might be, he was sure that there had been something he wanted to ask Lyn Goddard, but he could not think what it had been.

He knew that the way to deal with that sort of problem was to stop thinking about it, because once his mind was really off the subject, the answer would probably come to him all of a sudden, in the middle of something quite removed from it. But it was difficult to stop brooding about it. Accepting the bundle of manuscript from Colin, he said he would take it upstairs to his room and start reading it at once. Going upstairs, he settled down in the easy chair in his bedroom to read, then almost at once thought that he would be much more comfortable—if he had to stay up for he did not know how long, reading pages of handwriting which might well be as indecipherable as his own—if he changed into pyjamas and dressing-gown.

He left his shoes—which he had kicked off when he came in from his trip into Rockford—in the middle of the carpet, but kept on his socks, which he preferred to bedroom slippers. Then, instead of returning to the chair, he lay down on the bed, switching on the bedside lamp and arranging the pillows behind his head in a comfortable position for reading.

He need not have been afraid that the script would be illegible, for Lucas Dearden's handwriting, though small, was immaculately neat. Andrew began to feel that it was the handwriting of a vain man, a man who took pride in his ability to produce something so unnecessarily perfect. But that might be a reaction, Andrew realised, because of his recognition of his own scrawling inadequacy.

Apart from that, he soon began to find the book incredibly dull. At least the first third of it was devoted to a detailed tracing back of three generations of Lucas Dearden's forbears, who somehow, it appeared, had been connected with an earl. He did not appear to have been a very distinguished earl. He had taken no part in politics or the army, had not been a gambler who had lost his family's fortune, or a notorious roué, or been in any way dramatic. He had simply been a quiet, unassuming aristocrat, who farmed his acres and once a year took his family for a holiday to Switzerland. And Lucas's grandfather, who had been vaguely connected with this good man, had become a vicar in a country village where according to Lucas he had been deeply loved until, unfortunately for the family, he had read Herbert Spencer and had become an agnostic. "And by an agnostic," his grandson had quoted him as saying, "I mean one who, while exploring the knowable, pauses reverently—*reverently,* mind—on the threshold of the unknowable." He had of course had to resign his living, but soon afterwards a grand-aunt had conveniently died and he had been able to spend his years of religious doubt in comparative comfort, leaving a competence to his son; at all events, by the time that Lucas had appeared on the scene and had required an education, the family had been able to afford to send him to Winchester and Christchurch, after which he had entered on his own brilliant career.

Andrew, turning a page, gave a deep sigh. If Lucas Dearden had had the least gift for it, he could have made all this tale charming and fascinating, instead of merely a plodding exercise in name-dropping. Perhaps, Andrew thought, as he continued to read in spite of an increasing inclination to sleep, things would liven up a bit once Dearden reached the time when he had become eminent himself. But if anything it grew worse. Perhaps it was a fear of libel that made his description of the trials in which he had been involved sound drearily flat and undramatic; or perhaps the trouble was that he had made his reputation by eloquence, and eloquence does not transfer very well to paper unless the writer has remarkable literary ability or a competent ghost. Wit, which might have saved him, had never been Dearden's strong point, and it had been beyond him to convey the gesture, the throb in his voice, the flash of his eyes, which had once moved juries.

By the time Andrew came to the end of the manuscript, which he faithfully finished without much skipping, he was almost convinced that the law must be a very dull profession.

He had found a brief reference to the Waterman trial, but this was one of the parts that had mostly been crossed out. It was easily legible, however, and even if all of it had been left in the final version of the memoirs, Andrew could not see how it could have done any harm to anyone. There was nothing there that had not appeared in all the newspapers at the time of the trial, and he had a feeling that it had been deleted more because Thomas Waterman had been a man of no consequence and the evidence against him so overwhelming that there had been nothing notable about having him convicted. And anyway, how could Waterman have known that he had been even briefly mentioned in the memoirs, or indeed that Dearden was writing such a thing?

After he had laid the book aside, taken off his dressing-gown (stumbling over the shoes that he had left in the middle of the carpet), got into bed and turned off the light, Andrew toyed for a little while with the idea that Waterman might somehow be in touch with Dearden's literary agent. Dearden, after all, had had an appointment with him on the day after he had reached London, and presumably had cancelled this by telephone before starting for home. Henry Haslam, therefore, might not have been the only person who had known that Dearden was returning to Upper Cullonden. His agent most probably had known it. And he, moved by sympathy for Nicholas—who by now was a friend as well as a client—might by some means have communicated with Waterman and urged him to blow up Sir Lucas to the obvious advantage of Nicholas, and also himself and even some misguided publisher.

Andrew was half asleep before this thought formed itself hazily in his brain, confused because the words of an old Negro song, which had been popular when he was young, had started to weave through his thoughts.

I got shoes,
You got shoes,
All God's children got shoes,
When I get to Heaven goin' to kick off my shoes . . .

No, there was a misquotation somewhere there. It came of his bad habit of kicking off shoes and leaving them lying wherever he happened to have done so. It was all very well to do that when he was at home, but in someone else's house he really ought to be tidier. But at least he seemed to have escaped from Scott for the moment. Only briefly, however, for, by the time that he fell asleep he was possessed by the lines:

Heap on the wood!—the wind is chill,
But let it whistle as it will,
We'll keep our Christmas merry still . . .

Tomorrow was Christmas Day. No, it was today. The time was nearly two o'clock. And it had not been the heaping on of wood that had set that atrocious fire blazing in the lane, it had been a petrol tank exploding . . .

Sleep came as a blessed release, to be broken at last only by Jonathan appearing in his room with his breakfast tray.

"Merry Christmas," Jonathan said in a doleful tone.

"Merry Christmas," Andrew echoed him. "But really you shouldn't trouble, bringing me my breakfast like this. I can't help feeling it's a shocking luxury."

"It's no trouble," Jonathan said. "As a matter of fact, when we have people staying here Mum rather likes it if they don't mind breakfast in bed. Then she and Dad can sit over theirs in peace, reading the newspapers—though there isn't one this morning, of course, being Christmas—without feeling they ought to entertain anybody." He looked at the heap of manuscript on the bedside table. "Did you really read that yesterday evening?"

"Yes," Andrew said.

"The whole of it?"

"Yes."

"And what did you think of it?"

"I don't think I'm going to give any opinion till everyone else has read it." Andrew had heaved himself up in the bed, and Jonathan placed the tray on his knees. "Are you going to read it yourself?"

"Do you think I ought to?"

"I should say if your parents read it, that ought to be adequate."

"Perhaps I'll read it, all the same."

Jonathan left the room, and Andrew reached for the piece of cheese with which he had been thoughtfully supplied, before pouring out his coffee.

When he went downstairs about an hour later he took with him the presents that he had brought with him, without, however, having gone to the trouble of wrapping them up in special Christmas wrapping paper. He had brought a bottle of Glenlivet for Colin, a box of chocolates for Dorothea and a book-token for Jonathan. The book-token, Andrew felt, had been a serious failure of imagination on his part, but although he had known Jonathan since his childhood, he really knew very little about him now and had no idea what sort of gift might truly appeal to him. A book-token seemed safe.

But when he handed his presents over to Dorothea and she responded by giving him a fairly large parcel wrapped in paper of red and gold, dotted all over with Christmas trees, and he found that it contained a sweater in a very attractive shade of grey with an intricate pattern of soft blue, which she confessed that she had knitted herself, he felt that his own gifts were niggardly. Returning to his bedroom, he tried on the sweater and found that it fitted perfectly.

When he had taken his presents down with him, he had added Lucas Dearden's manuscript to them, handing that over to Colin, who, like Jonathan, had wanted to know Andrew's opinion of it. As before, he said that he did not want to give an opinion until at least Colin had read it; on coming downstairs again, wearing the grey sweater, feeling very good in it and prepared to tell Dorothea quite sincerely how much he liked it, Andrew found Colin already reading by the sitting-room fire.

The absence of a newspaper was irritating, but the copy of *The Economist* on which Andrew had started the evening before the bomb, was still in the room. He settled down with it, doing his best not to disturb Colin. Presently a scent of cooking reached the room, and after a while Jonathan came in, saying that it was time for drinks and did everyone want sherry.

Dorothea joined them and said that if only she had known how things were going to turn out, making it impossible to go to the Deardens, she would have bought a turkey for themselves; but that anyway the sirloin looked good and would very likely be better than the frozen turkey, which was the only kind that she could have bought in the supermarket at the last moment.

Accepting sherry from Jonathan and looking at Colin, she said, "What are you making of that?"

"So far," Colin said, "absolutely nothing at all. It's quite extraordinarily dull."

"Is there anything in it about Thomas Waterman?" she asked.

"I've come on one passage about the case," Colin said. "There's a mention of the fact that Waterman caught his wife in bed with a man, that the man, before bolting, gave him a beating and that Waterman then beat up his wife and killed her." He looked at Andrew. "Is there anything more about the case later on?"

"No," Andrew said. "I don't think Dearden found it interesting enough to write about it."

"The one odd thing, it seems to me," Colin said, "is that if Waterman had given himself up and pleaded guilty, he'd probably have got a still lighter sentence than he did. There was plenty of provocation. But he put up a dogged defence, and though Lucas doesn't mention it here, there's the fact that he shouted threats from the dock at the judge and Lucas. So he may be sufficiently unbalanced to have planted a bomb to kill Lucas. But we still don't know how he could have known that Lucas would be driving along the lane at the time he was. I know there's the theory that Waterman could have been in touch with Henry and got information from him, but I don't really believe it."

"I wonder if the police will arrest him," Dorothea said.

"More likely take him in for questioning," Jonathan said, "if he hasn't already scarpered."

"Anyway, let's remember it's Christmas and try to enjoy ourselves," Dorothea said. "More sherry, everyone?"

If they did not quite succeed in enjoying themselves with any of the Christmas spirit, they did presently enjoy an excellent meal. Dorothea had insisted that dinner should be at midday and not in the evening. There was smoked salmon, then roast beef with roast potatoes and cauliflower, followed by the mince pies which she had tried unsuccessfully the evening before to tempt people to eat. They were delicious. They drank Côte du Rhone and afterwards coffee and Cointreau. After that Jonathan and Andrew attacked the washing-up, while Colin returned to Lucas Dearden's manuscript and Dorothea settled down with some knitting on the sitting-room sofa, her feet up as usual.

While they were doing the washing-up Andrew studied Jonathan's profile as he bent over the sink. He was certainly a very good-looking young man, and had a good deal of charm and spirit. So could Dorothea be right, Andrew wondered, that he and Gwen were in love with one another? And could that be Jonathan's reason for continuing to live here with his parents? Was it simply that he and Gwen could meet so easily?

Andrew did not really think that likely. He thought that Jonathan simply liked living at home. Apart from his apparent affection for his parents, he was comfortably housed, well fed, and had far fewer domestic worries than he would have if he lived by himself in a flat in Rockford. Perhaps if he had a place of his own he would have a little more opportunity to meet Gwen privately, but not really so very much. Her husband did not go out to work. He spent all day at home. If she was constantly driving into Rockford, he would soon notice and begin to wonder what she was doing there. But even if such a thing were to happen, would he take to murder—and by a manner so crude as a bomb?

Polishing a glass carefully, Andrew said, "Jonathan, have you any enemies?"

"Ah," Jonathan said, "you've thought of that, have you?"

"That perhaps you were the intended victim the other night. You'd thought that of it, had you?"

"Oh yes, I thought of it almost at once."

"Because you've been half-expecting something of the sort?"

"Good God, no. Only for the simple reason that no one could have known when Lucas would get here, and half the village knows when I drive along the lane."

"You haven't answered my question; have you any enemies?"

Jonathan was washing up plates and putting them into a rack to dry.

After a moment he said, "I expect I have. Haven't most of us? In your academic days, didn't you sometimes feel that there was someone in your department who wished you'd drop dead?"

"But they never did anything about it."

"So you think that feeling wasn't very real?"

"I suppose so."

"Well, that's how I really feel about it too. There are people whom I've got across in my job. I know it and I know they wouldn't be sorry if I quietly disappeared. But so far as I know, all they're thinking of is how satisfactory it would be if I got a job elsewhere. But aren't there plenty of lunatics wandering around among us whom everyone is ready to swear are the most normal and pleasant sort of people, until they get hold of a gun and suddenly start shooting up everyone in sight? I'm afraid I don't know much about that sort of thing, and I wouldn't be good at diagnosing anything of the kind, but in a way it does seem the simplest explanation of what's happened, doesn't it?"

"But there's no special person you're afraid of?"

"No, I can't honestly say there is."

"All the same, having thought of yourself as the intended victim of that bomb, aren't you at all frightened?"

"I'm scared as hell."

Jonathan's voice had suddenly risen a little in pitch, and for the first time Andrew began to feel that it might be true that the young man was frightened. Yet he had tried to make what he said sound like a joke. Andrew wondered what the truth was. Was he truly scared, or did he somehow know that he had not been the intended target?

"Of course you're going to tell this to the police," he said.

"Oh, I don't think so," Jonathan replied. "They'll think of it themselves, and if they come along and question me then I can only tell them what I've just told you."

"Which I believe is only about half the truth," Andrew said.

"Half a truth is better than no truth," Jonathan declared and laughed.

Andrew gave up at that point. He and Jonathan finished the washing-up and rejoined Colin and Dorothea in the sitting-room.

Colin was just reading the last few pages of Lucas Dearden's memoirs, and took no notice of Andrew, who went to the window and looked out at the damply colourless garden, wondering if he should go for a walk. He was not used to a heavy meal at midday, and knew that if he sat down he would soon nod off to sleep. But perhaps there would be a film worth watching on television. He was thinking of asking Dorothea what she would feel about having the television on while she knitted, when Colin spoke to him.

"Andrew, you don't think there's anything of any interest whatever in all this stuff, do you?"

"Is that your feeling?" Andrew asked.

"I really never realised the old man had so much dullness in him," Colin said. "He was quite amusing to talk to, you know. Of course, fearfully vain and given to telling you the same joke over and over again as if he'd only just thought of it, but I can't see that there's anything here that could alarm anyone at all."

"That was my own reaction," Andrew said.

"Then I needn't read it—thank the Lord for that!" Dorothea exclaimed. "There aren't any deadly secrets that I might fathom? I'll do a job on it if you think I ought, but I'll be so thankful if I needn't."

"I can't see why you should if you don't want to," Colin said. "You agree with me, don't you, Andrew?"

"Yes," Andrew said. "He ought to have got Nicholas to write it up for him. He'd probably have made it very readable."

"You know, he always rather despised Nicholas," Dorothea said. "He used to show it by saying unnecessarily sarcastic things about him. Erica was the member of the family he really cared for. Of course she's really very lovely and I believe she looks rather like her mother, who died years ago. Is there much about Lady Dearden in the memoirs?"

"Hardly anything at all," Colin said, "but I don't criticize him for that. It's all pretty impersonal. Her death is only mentioned as one of the things which drove him on in his ambition in the law. And there's very little about Nicholas and Erica. He speaks with satisfaction of Erica's marriage to Henry, because Henry was ambitious like himself and successful. But he seems almost embarrassed by his having a son who's made a career out of writing spy stories. And he never mentions Gwen at all."

The doorbell rang.

"I'll go," Jonathan said, and went quickly out of the room.

A moment later he returned with a visitor. It was Thomas Waterman.

FIVE

COLIN TRIED TO TAKE the man's raincoat from him, but he kept it clutched around him as if he feared it might be cold in the room; or perhaps it was merely to show that he had no intention of staying more than a few minutes. He held his black beret in one hand, his grey hair hanging greasily over his ears. When Colin had told Dorothea that this was Mr. Waterman, and had invited him to sit down, he sat on the very edge of a chair, as if to make it plain that this was to be a very short visit.

"They're setting me up for murder again," he announced.

This was embarrassing. No one said anything.

He repeated it in a louder tone, as if he feared that he had not been heard. "They're setting me up for murder."

"I'm sorry, but I don't see how we can help," Colin said.

The man waved his beret at the door. "There's a man out there waiting till I come out. They're following me wherever I go."

"I suppose that must give you an uncomfortable sort of feeling," Colin said.

"I tell you, they're setting me up for murder."

"Have they any evidence?"

"As if they care about that! They've my record. That's enough for them. You probably think I'm a murderer too."

"I don't think any of us have very definite opinions," Colin said. "But you came to us for some reason, I imagine."

"I want to talk to that man, whoever he is," Waterman said, pointing at Andrew and glaring at him with his strange, crooked eyes.

"He's Professor Basnett," Colin said. "A friend who's spending Christmas with us."

"The man I talked to the other morning," Waterman stated, and seemed to expect someone to contradict him.

Andrew said, "That's correct. For a moment you seemed to think I might be Sir Lucas Dearden."

"I expected to see him, but as soon as I saw you I knew you weren't him. Isn't that right?"

"Yes, I think it is," Andrew said.

"Not that I was sure, just for a second. I didn't really know what he'd look like after all this time. And the only times I saw him he was dressed up in a wig and all that, and I can't say I was quite myself. I'd too much else on my mind, and it was all so long ago. If you'd said you were Dearden, I'd have believed you."

"But I didn't," Andrew said.

"No, you didn't."

"So how can I help you?"

"You don't much want to help me, do you? It's easiest for you to believe I'm a murderer. It's easiest for everyone."

"If you aren't," Andrew said, "what did you come down here for?"

Waterman twisted his beret between his hands. He brooded for a moment.

"I wanted to meet the man," he said. "I wanted to talk to

him, that was all. I've had time to do a lot of thinking in the
last few years, and in the early days there was nothing I
wanted so much as to get my hands round his throat and
throttle him. I used to lie awake in bed and dream about
doing it. Then after a time I got tired of it, and I saw that
what I had to do when I got out was to put it all behind me
and get him and the bloody old judge out of my system, or
there wasn't much point in getting out of goal. Then the
judge died, so I couldn't see him, but Dearden was living
here, comfortably retired. And I thought I could come here
and talk to him and see what kind of man he was who could
do what he did to me."

"Are you saying you were innocent of the murder of your
wife?" Colin asked.

"No need to do that now, is there?" Waterman said. "I've
paid for it. I can say what I like about it and no one can do
anything more to me. No, I did it and never been sorry for it
either. Sorry I ever married her, yes, knowing pretty well as
I did what she was, but thinking, as I expect other men have
thought before me, that I could straighten her out if I cared
for her enough and gave her security and all that. I should
have known you can't change people. Funny thing, she
hadn't really much use for sex. Always seemed to be looking
for something she couldn't find in one man after another.
Frigid as hell all the time. That's what a lot of these tarts are
like, so I've been told. I was told a lot of things in prison I
didn't know when I went there. Don't they call them univer-
sities of crime? Isn't that the fashionable thing to say about
them nowadays? Not that I ever learnt anything that's been
much use to me. I didn't learn how to make bombs. I didn't
learn how to make sure I'd a good alibi when there was a
smell of murder in the air. I didn't learn how to talk nice and
politely to the police when they start shouting at me."

"But you think that I can help you in some way," Andrew
said.

Waterman edged even further forward on his chair. It

looked as if he were ready to leap up from it, perhaps at Andrew, perhaps for the door.

"Did you or did you not tell me that Dearden was in London?" he demanded.

"Yes, I did," Andrew replied.

"And you said you didn't know when he'd be back."

"Yes."

"Then how the hell was I to know he'd be coming back that evening? First I didn't know he'd be away, so how was I to know about his coming back?"

"That's what's puzzling a good many people at the moment," Andrew said. "How did anyone know?"

"Oh, they knew in the other house all right. He phoned them to say he was coming."

"Apparently not. There were no phone calls that day."

"Who says?"

"Mr. and Mrs. Dearden and a visitor who's staying with them, a Miss Goddard."

"And why should you believe them? Oughtn't you to be asking yourselves, is it probable?" Waterman started to massage his knees with his big, bony hands. His crooked eyes still dwelt intently on Andrew's face. "I'd no motive for killing that old devil. Like I was telling you, I outgrew that long ago. The only motive I could have had is if I fancied another long spell in prison and thought it might as well be Dearden I finished off as anyone else. And I may come round to that yet. Life outside hasn't been much better than inside. I'd no worries there, no need to think about where the next meal was coming from, no getting the brush-off when I tried to get a job, no need to queue up for my unemployment benefit." He stood up suddenly, tall and very thin, his raincoat still tightly clutched about him. "Sorry, I didn't mean to get talking. I'm not trying to make you sorry for me. I just want to know if you'll tell the police you didn't tell me when Dearden was expected home."

"I think I've told them that already," Andrew said.

"Just a minute." Jonathan stood in front of the door as Waterman moved towards it. "Has it occurred to you that the bomb may not have been meant for Sir Lucas? I wonder if you can prove that no one gave you that bomb and paid you to plant it in the lane to blow up somebody else."

"Jonathan!" Dorothea yelped. "Do you know what you're saying?"

"Of course I do," he said. "And so do you and so do the police. What I'm advising Mr. Waterman to do is to stop worrying about who could have known Lucas was coming home and concentrate on proving that he's never been in touch with anyone who wanted to blow me up. His coming here, a well-known murderer like him, just when a murder was set to happen, seems to me a bit too much of a coincidence unless it had somehow been arranged for him to be the fall-guy. Isn't that the word for it?"

Waterman gave him a hard stare, then thrust past him out of the house. They heard the bang of the front door behind him.

Jonathan went to his mother, stooped over her and gave her a kiss.

"I'm sorry, Mum, I didn't mean to worry you, but you'd thought of all that yourself, hadn't you?" he said. "I think it'd be best for us all if we accept that the bomb was almost certainly meant for me."

"I'd never have thought of what you said to that man," Dorothea said. "I mean that he was, well, someone else's instrument. I thought he was quite innocent."

"Perhaps he is," Jonathan said. "I said he may have been got down here by someone just to be a useful suspect."

"Then why hasn't he said what brought him here?" she demanded.

"Ah yes, why? And who hates me quite enough to try a thing like that?"

Colin's plump face was uncharacteristically sombre. "If you're right," he said, "it was a very carefully planned, cold-blooded murder, worked out some time ago. No, you know, Jonathan, when I think about it carefully, I don't believe a word of it."

Jonathan gave a sudden laugh, as if he were pleased by what his father had just said.

"That's a relief, though I don't know why you don't," he said. "It all sounded pretty convincing to me. So we're back, as always, to who knew Lucas was coming down."

"I suppose there's a possibility," Andrew said, "that the bomb was meant for Colin or Dorothea."

This, as he had intended, produced mirth. No one thought even for a moment that there could be any truth in it. Dorothea laid down her knitting and stood up.

"I'll get tea," she said and went out.

A little while later Andrew said, "I suppose someone ought to take that manuscript back to the Deardens. I'll do it, if you like."

He had a feeling that it would be a good thing for the Cahills to have a little time to themselves, without even as old a friend as he was there to hear their discussion.

"Will you?" Colin said. "Thanks very much. But all you can say to them is that it appears to be entirely innocuous."

"I wonder if they'll be glad of that, or not," Jonathan said. "I mean, if you'd spotted some good old clue in it, it might have helped."

Dorothea had picked it up, and though she had not settled down to read it, she had been leafing through it.

"Have you noticed that page 96 is missing?" she asked.

"No. Is it?" Colin asked.

"Yes, it just caught my eye. It goes from 95 to 97."

"I didn't notice it," he said. "Did you, Andrew?"

"No." Andrew took the manuscript from Dorothea and looked at the pages that she indicated. All the pages were numbered neatly at the top with a number enclosed in a little circle. As she had pointed out, page 96 was missing. "But it reads quite coherently as it is," he said. "Perhaps it was just a slip."

He held the manuscript out to Colin, who looked at it and nodded.

"Makes perfect sense as it is," he said.

On page 95 there was a mention of the fact that Lucas's daughter Erica had just become engaged, and on page 97 it went on to say that Henry Haslam had recently become senior partner of the firm of accountants for whom he worked, followed by a few words of commendation. As Colin had said, it made perfectly good sense.

"Well, we'll never know what was on page 96, if there ever was one," Jonathan said after he too had looked at the manuscript. "I think Andrew was right, Lucas just made a slip numbering his pages, though I suppose he might have torn it out for some reason and thrown it away."

"Erica was always her father's favourite, was she?" Andrew said.

"I think she was," Colin replied. "You think Nicholas felt that? That it's another thing against him at the moment?"

"I was just wondering if Dearden said something disparaging about Nicholas on that missing page, then had second thoughts about it and tore it out," Andrew said. "But really I've no opinion about it at all. Shall I take the manuscript back now?"

It was handed over to him very willingly. He went upstairs and changed his shoes, then walked out into the lane and along it to the Deardens' gate.

The front door was opened to him by Lyn Goddard.

"Ah, you've brought the manuscript back," she said as she invited him in. "Have you read it?"

"Yes, and so has Colin," he said. "We seem to agree about it."

"That it's a wretched dull thing?"

She led him into the high, gracious drawing-room with its incongruous modern furniture. A fire was burning on the hearth of the fine old Adam fireplace, casting flickering shadows about the panelled walls, but there was no light on in the room. She pressed a couple of switches and light sprang on in several lamps. There was no sign of Nicholas or Gwen. Andrew wondered if Lyn had been sitting there alone, dreaming in the early winter dusk—it would have been too dark to read—or if she had only just come downstairs when she heard his ring.

Taking the manuscript from him and putting it on a table, she gestured to a chair and sat down herself.

"Nicholas is lying down," she said. "He had to go and make a formal identification of what was left of his father today, Christmas or not, and he came home and straight away started vomiting. Vomiting several times. It must have been a terrible thing for him to have to do, and Nicholas is really very sensitive."

It sounded as if she herself might have made the identification without needing more than perhaps a small whisky after it.

"And how's Gwen?" Andrew asked.

"I don't know," she said. "She's been gone all day. She drove up to London to see Erica. I should think she'll be back any time now."

"How is Erica?"

"Doing pretty well, I believe. It was a nasty accident, but luckily not too serious."

"Lyn, there's something I want to ask you." Andrew had promptly remembered on seeing her what it was that he had wanted to ask her. His mind had been a blank on the subject until a short time ago, when he had seen Dorothea's Christmas tree with its decoration of cards. But now he knew what it had been. "I believe, when you came down by train, you were writing Christmas cards."

"It's true, I was," she said. "I've kept meaning to do it ever since the beginning of the month, and I actually bought them a couple of weeks ago, but I kept forgetting about them, or finding something I had to do that seemed more urgent. And of course they'll arrive days too late, because you know how slow the post is around Christmas time. But I did scribble them in the train. Why?" She gave a puzzled frown. "Do they matter in some way?"

"I'm only wondering when you posted them," Andrew said. "Or didn't you post them at all? Have you still got them?"

"Oh no, I posted them."

"At the station?"

"No. Oh—!" She had understood what he was asking her. "I posted them as soon as we got here. There's a letter-box at the end of the lane. I noticed it as we were driving along, and before I took my things upstairs or did any unpacking I went straight out and popped them all into it. And that means I was out of the house for about five minutes, and someone could have rung up while I was out and I shouldn't have heard the telephone. Isn't that what you're thinking about?"

"It's true, it is," Andrew admitted. "You were so positive no one could have rung up to tell the Deardens Sir Lucas was on his way home, but if a call had come through during the short time you were out of the house you wouldn't have known about it."

"And so Nicholas could have planted the bomb to kill his father? Always supposing he had a bomb handy." There was mockery in her tone.

"Suppose he had," Andrew said.

She looked shocked at the seriousness of his tone.

"It sounds to me very improbable," she said.

"So it does to me," Andrew admitted. "But the improbable sometimes happens. And I thought I'd just ask you about it."

"Well, I did go out and the telephone could have rung while I was gone," she said, "that's obvious. But didn't it happen at the wrong time of day? I mean, I've been told Erica had her accident about midday, but it wasn't long after midday that the Deardens brought me here from the station.

So if Henry rang up then to tell them that Lucas was on his way home, it would have meant that Henry had done it almost as soon as he had the news of the accident himself, just when he was talking to the police and seeing about getting Erica into hospital and all that sort of thing. Isn't that unlikely?"

"Suppose it was Dearden himself who rang up," Andrew said.

She nodded. "Yes, I can just imagine that. The first thing he'd have thought of when he heard that Erica wouldn't be available to look after him over Christmas would have been that the most comfortable thing for him to do would be to go home. But I'm not sure that he'd have bothered to telephone. I think he'd probably simply have left Henry to cope with everything and got into his car and driven home."

"You didn't like him," Andrew said. "That's evident."

She gave a sigh. "Isn't it difficult to say that of the dead? Specially of someone so horribly dead. If he'd died in his bed, say after a long illness, and we'd all been agreed it was a merciful release for everyone, I don't think I'd have hesitated to say he was an old bastard. Or perhaps I should. I don't know. He was never unkind to me and always made me feel I was welcome here. But he was selfish and demanding and exploited Nicholas and Gwen in every way that occurred to him. All the same, if you think that Nicholas murdered him, it won't do. Nicholas isn't that kind of man."

"And Gwen?" he said.

She gave a start of surprise. "*Gwen?*"

"It doesn't take a lot of muscular strength to plant a bomb in a lane," he said, "and there've been plenty of woman terrorists."

"What an extraordinary idea," she said, yet she did not sound much disturbed by it. "But you know, I think if she'd wanted to kill him she'd have put some insecticide in his soup or something like that. That's how I'd have done it myself. You've wondered about that, of course. You've wondered if I could have had any possible motive for killing Lucas."

"That's the kind of thing I sometimes think about," he said, "but I don't usually take it very seriously."

"I suppose we all do it from time to time." She stirred in her chair, moving her gaze from his face to the manuscript on the table. "You say you've read that thing."

He nodded.

"And you thought it pretty dreary stuff. But was that all you thought?"

"Is there anything more that I ought to have thought?"

"I don't think so. I've only glanced through it, but Nicholas said that he doubted if it would ever get published unless the old man paid for it himself."

"Did Dearden know that he thought that?"

"I don't think so. Nicholas would never have risked saying a thing like that to his father. I think in his way he was always rather afraid of him. He could be wickedly sarcastic, you know. It could be vicious. I don't want to give you the idea that anyone as quiet and gentle as Nicholas could carry out a particularly brutal murder, but I do think, though I've a feeling, as I've just said, that one shouldn't say such things, that he'll be better off now."

"Financially?"

"Oh yes, of course financially. But that isn't what I meant."

"Tell me, have you or Nicholas noticed that page 96 in the manuscript is missing?"

Her gaze came sharply back to him. "No. Is it?"

"It appears to be," Andrew said. "Yet it reads as if there'd been nothing left out. It could be that in writing Dearden simply made a slip and wrote 97 after 95. Or it could be that he tore out a page and threw it away. Do you happen to know who typed it for him before he sent it to his agent?"

"I believe some woman in the village, someone who I believe had been somebody's secretary, then got married and

settled here, but welcomed the odd job of work. Is it important? Nicholas or Gwen would know, I expect."

"It might be important," Andrew said. "I don't know."

"I'll ask Nicholas about it and let you know."

But as she spoke, Nicholas came into the room. His thick
fair hair was dishevelled and the cardigan that he was wearing was wrongly buttoned, so that it looked as if he had tum-
bled off his bed, or wherever he had been lying down, without troubling to tidy himself. He looked startled at seeing
Andrew.

"I'm sorry," he said. "I didn't know you were here. I've
been trying to rest, but it doesn't really work, though I
haven't had much sleep the last night or two." He turned to
Lyn. "Gwen not back yet?"

"No," she said.

"I don't know why she went," he said with some petulance
in his voice. "There wasn't any need for it. Erica wouldn't
have been expecting her, after hearing what happened here."

"I suppose Henry did tell her," Lyn said. "But mightn't he
have felt she could be spared the shock for a few days of
knowing about it?"

"All the more reason why Gwen needn't have gone. But I
think Henry told Erica everything. Did I tell you he's probably coming down here tomorrow? He phoned just a little
while ago. Seemed to think he might be able to help us,
though I don't know how." He turned back to Andrew.
"Have you met Henry?"

Andrew shook his head.

"You haven't missed much, though there's no harm in
him," Nicholas said with an edge on his voice. He seemed to
be in a thoroughly bad humour.

"Your father seemed to think a good deal of him," Andrew
said.

"What? Oh, you've been reading that manuscript." Nicholas glanced towards it, then threw himself down in a chair.

"Yes, he says some reasonably complimentary things about him, doesn't he? Henry knew how to handle him."

"Of course you know there's a page missing from the manuscript," Andrew said.

"No. Is there?" Nicholas did not look much interested.

"The numbering of the pages goes from 95 to 97," Andrew told him. "It could have been a slip your father made as he was writing, or it could be that he decided to remove the page for some reason."

"I suppose that's odd," Nicholas said. "I read it through, but never noticed it. It makes sense as it is, doesn't it?"

"Yes, I read it straight on without noticing it myself. It was Dorothea who pointed it out."

Nicholas gave a slight shrug of his shoulders. "Probably isn't important anyway. What did you make of the whole thing?"

"Nothing much."

"No, he was very careful not to say anything about himself, wasn't he? Or about Erica or me, I'm glad to say."

"The missing page, if that's what it was, seems to have been about your brother-in-law. There's a mention on page 95 of your sister's engagement, then it goes on on 97 with the statement that Henry Haslam was senior partner in the firm he worked for."

Nicholas stood up and reached for the manuscript. He flicked the pages over.

"You're quite right, it's missing," he said, "but I'd guess it was just a mistake in the numbering. I wonder if it will get published now. If it's got out in a hurry the publicity at present might help it."

Andrew would not have expected him to sound as callous as he did. But the cause of that, he thought, might be simply that the stress of the last days had exhausted Nicholas's emotional capacities. His face was very pale and showed deeper lines than usual. He had never had the toughness for which his father had once been famous. Yet several people seemed inclined to think that he might be a murderer. But perhaps murder could be a last resort of weakness.

"I was asking Lyn who typed the manuscript," Andrew said. "She told me a woman in the village did it. Might she know anything about the missing page?"

"Doesn't seem likely," Nicholas said. "If it ever existed and if my father tore it out, he'd have done that before taking it to be typed, wouldn't he? She won't have seen it."

"No, that's true," Andrew agreed.

"But it was done by a woman called Mrs. Cambrey, who lives in a bungalow with the odd name of Elsinore, next to the church. Not that you need expect to meet a ghost walking on the battlements if you go there. I believe she and her husband thought of the name for their home because her name is Elsie and his is Norman. I believe a lot of people name their houses in that way, and sometimes it has some rather bizarre results." He had dropped back into his chair. "Now why the hell doesn't Gwen come home?"

Andrew stood up. He thought it possible that he might visit Elsinore, though not that evening, and perhaps by next day he might have lost the inclination to do so. But the puzzle of the missing page roused his curiosity and although he did what he could to control it, curiosity had always been a powerful part of his character. Nicholas showed him to the front door, opened it and, standing there looking out, said, "The lane's still roped off. Gwen will have to drive round by the village. I wonder how long it'll be before things get back to normal."

He sounded less callous now than sad, as if something that had been precious to him had been irremediably destroyed.

"Do the police know for sure yet if the bomb was planted in the lane," Andrew asked, "or if it was attached to your father's car, or put into it, in London?"

"Oh, it was in the lane," Nicholas answered. "They've found traces of explosive there. It was a land-mine of sorts. Anyone coming along could have been blown up. The lane's so narrow that whoever did it could be sure that anyone driving down along it would explode it. You've thought of that, I suppose."

"That it could have been meant for Jonathan? Yes, we've talked it over."

"Only somehow I don't think it was. Well, thank you for bringing the manuscript back." Nicholas turned back into the house and closed the door.

Andrew started down the drive towards the gate.

He had only gone a yard or so when a car stopped in the gateway and someone got out. It was too dark for him to see who it was, but the figure started walking back along the lane, perhaps towards the village or perhaps only to the house next door. The car turned in at the gate, and continued to the Deardens' garage. There was no reason why Andrew should linger, since this was certainly Gwen returning from London and she would have nothing to say to him, but he paused and after a moment she emerged from the garage and walked towards the door.

As she came close to him he could see her face in the light from one of the windows in the house, and it was certain that she must have seen him in the headlights of her car; yet she walked past him as if he were not there, a stiff, erect figure with eyes staring glassily out of the pallor of her face. Opening the door, she disappeared into the house.

He gave an unhappy sigh as he walked towards the gate. It was almost certain, he thought, that the figure whom he had seen get hurriedly out of the car had been Jonathan, and it was only a moment before he was sure of this, for Jonathan was standing near the door of the Cahills' house, waiting for him. As Andrew approached, Jonathan came a few steps towards him.

"So you saw us," he said.

"Yes," Andrew answered. "Does that matter?"

"Only that perhaps you needn't mention it to my parents,"

Jonathan said. "They knew I was going out, but they didn't know where."

"Where did you go, or is that a private matter too?" Andrew asked.

"Not really. I suppose actually I'll tell them about it myself." The porch light was on, but Andrew could not see much of Jonathan's face. "I've got some things I've got to think out. The fact is, Gwen phoned me from The Running Man and wanted me to meet her there. She'd been up to London to visit Erica, who seems to be doing all right, but as far as I can make out, between them they've come to the conclusion that Nicholas must have murdered his father, only they don't think it was his father he was trying to kill, it was me. And Gwen wanted to see me to implore me to go away. She thinks I'm in real danger. But she told me she won't give evidence against Nicholas, because he's her husband. She's very loyal to him."

"Has she any evidence to give?" Andrew asked.

"You mean solid evidence, not just some hysterical guesses?"

"Yes, that's what I mean."

"As a matter of fact, I asked her that and she wouldn't tell me. My impression is . . ." Jonathan paused and turned towards the door. As he turned the handle to open it, he added, "I believe she knows something. Something. I don't know what. But what would you do if you were me?"

"I'd be on the next plane to South America."

Jonathan laughed. "I knew you'd say something like that. I needn't have asked you. But you see, it isn't a joke to me."

He pushed the door open.

"Actually not to me either," Andrew said as he stepped inside. "If you don't like South America, there are still the Antipodes."

Jonathan stood still in the hall, looking at him with a perplexed frown on his normally cheerful, confident face.

"I believe you really mean that," he said.

"But then I'm no hero and I'm not in love with anyone," Andrew replied. "That may make a difference."

"I'm not in love with anyone either," Jonathan said quickly. "If you're thinking of Gwen and me—" Just at that moment Dorothea called out from the sitting-room.

"Jonathan, is that you?"

"Yes," he called back. Then he dropped his voice to almost a whisper in Andrew's ear. "They think I've been having a drink with a friend in the village. They don't know it was Gwen. But I'll think about South America."

He leapt up the stairs and Andrew heard the door of his bedroom slam as he went into it.

Andrew went into the sitting-room. Colin gave him sherry and Dorothea told him that supper was waiting for him. There was going to be cold roast beef with biscuits and cheese. Andrew sat down, wondering what he ought to say to them. He had given Jonathan no promise not to tell them that Gwen had been the friend with whom he had been having a drink.

"I don't think I'll ever make mince pies again," Dorothea said. "There are still some over, but all they'll ever do to me is remind me of these awful days. Had they anything to say about the manuscript over at the Deardens', Andrew?"

"Nothing much, except that they told me who typed it for Dearden," he answered. "A woman called Mrs. Cambrey. I've been wondering if she could know anything about that missing page."

"I suppose it's possible," Colin said. "It might be worth asking her."

"Will you do it?" Andrew asked.

"Wouldn't it be better if you did? She knows me. She'll think I'm just being inquisitive. If you handle it the right way she might even think you're connected with the police and that she ought to tell you everything she knows."

"Face it, that's probably nothing."

"Of course. All the same, its being missing is just a little odd. It somehow isn't in character for Lucas simply to have made a slip in numbering the pages. You know how neat it all was and how carefully he'd crossed out all the bits he wanted to delete. Still, I admit anyone can act out of character once in a while. But there can't be any harm in asking her if she knows anything."

Andrew nodded, making up his mind that next morning he would call on Mrs. Cambrey, but his thoughts were really on Jonathan. How deeply involved was he with Gwen Dearden, and how much did that mean to Nicholas?

Jonathan came down for supper, but then returned upstairs while Colin, Dorothea and Andrew watched a film on television. They all went to bed early, Andrew settling down for a time to his Rex Stout before switching off his light, half-dreading to do so because he felt that in the darkness he would once more be assailed by the vision of the flames in the lane, the blazing car and the charred figure inside it.

However, he fell asleep fairly soon, after making up his mind that after breakfast next day he would visit Mrs. Cambrey. It seemed a futile thing to do, but as Colin had said, it was unlikely to do any harm.

He was woken in the morning by Dorothea coming suddenly into his room. She was not carrying a breakfast tray and she left the door open behind her. Her face was pale with shock.

"He's gone, Andrew—Jonathan's gone!" she cried. "His bed hasn't been slept in and he's taken a suitcase and his car. What's happened? Where has he gone? What in God's name are we to do about it?"

SIX

ANDREW WAS ALARMED. He was not used to having his advice followed, and so expeditiously. He was not much used either to giving advice. It seemed to him a very dangerous practice. On the few occasions when he himself had followed someone else's advice, something had generally gone wrong. But where had Jonathan gone?

Still dopey from sleep, he inquired, "Has he taken his passport?"

"His passport! Oh, my God, I didn't think of that!"

Dorothea shot out of the room.

While she was gone Andrew got out of bed and put on his dressing-gown. He felt as if something were the matter with his head. It felt thick and strange and stupid. After only two or three minutes Dorothea was back.

"I can't be sure," she said, her voice shaking. "I thought he kept it in a drawer of the desk in his room, and it isn't there. But I haven't really searched yet. He may simply have moved it. Why did you say that, Andrew?"

"Just that he and I were talking about his going away yesterday evening," he answered. "But of course I never dreamt of his doing anything so precipitate. Hasn't he left you a message of some kind?"

"Nothing at all. Why did you talk about his going away?"

Why had they? For a moment Andrew's mind was a blank. Then he remembered.

"Oh, of course it was because of the possibility that the bomb was meant for him. You talked about that yourself."

"Yes, but imagine, not to let us know what he meant to do!" She seemed about to say something more, then turned and went running downstairs.

Andrew washed, shaved and got dressed. No one was thinking that morning of bringing him breakfast in his room. Going downstairs, he found Dorothea sitting broodingly at the table in the kitchen, nursing a cup of coffee in both hands. When he appeared she got up and fetched another cup and filled it with coffee, tipped some cornflakes into a bowl and pushed it towards him, then sat down again and swallowed some coffee that was evidently so hot that she choked over it. She had no thought of supplying him with cheese.

"Where's Colin?" he asked. "Does he know Jonathan's vanished?"

"Oh yes, it was he who found Jonathan had taken his car," she said. "He's gone round to the Deardens to ask them if they know anything."

"Why should they?"

"Well, one's got to do something. I don't expect they do know anything."

"Perhaps you'll get a message from Jonathan later on."

"Do you think so? You mean, he might telephone from wherever he's gone."

"Or perhaps he'll simply come back. He may have found last night that he didn't feel like trying to sleep, and he thought of driving off somewhere on his own to think things out."

"But you asked about his passport."

"I was only half awake."

"You don't think he's suddenly gone off abroad somewhere?"

"If he did, what would he use for money?"

She thrust her fingers through her hair, clawing at her head as if that might help her to think more clearly.

"I don't know, but perhaps he had quite a lot. I mean, he might have got next month's salary in advance, because of the holiday, and if he'd cashed the cheque . . ." She stopped, frowning. The lines across her forehead deepened. "But why should he have cashed it unless he was planning some days ago to go away, and that isn't likely, is it? His salary usually gets paid straight into his bank account, and he gives me a cheque for his share of the housekeeping. He always insisted on doing that as soon as he started earning some money. And I suppose he gets out some ready cash for himself from time to time, but I don't think it's ever very much, certainly not enough to go abroad with. Though he does have one of those credit cards . . ." She stopped again. "You don't seriously think he's done anything like that, do you?" The thought of the credit card had shocked her. Her tone implored him to reassure her.

"It seems to me there's nothing we can do but wait and see," he said, "unless you want to tell the police he's gone missing."

"No—oh no, that would be the worst thing we could do! I mean, if he just wants to be left in peace for a little, we don't want them thinking he's run away from them for some reason. And it would be difficult to explain the actual reason why we think he might have done it."

"I'm not sure that it would," Andrew said. "I think that man Roland may have thought, all on his own, that Jonathan might have been the target for that bomb. And I think if he doesn't appear fairly soon, or send you some message, it might actually be best to tell the police what's happened. But I don't suppose it'll do any harm to wait a little."

Just then they heard the sound of the front door opening and closing, then footsteps coming towards the kitchen. Dorothea had looked up with hopeful expectancy, but the footsteps were unmistakably Colin's.

When he came into the kitchen his face was sombre.

"Any coffee left?" he asked.

"Yes. Yes, of course." Dorothea sprang up to fetch another cup from the cupboard. "What's happened, Colin? They don't know anything, do they?"

"Well, that's a bit of a problem," Colin said. He sat down at the table and sipped the coffee that she gave him. "Yes, quite a bit of a problem."

"What do you mean?" Her anxiety was mounting sharply at his obvious reluctance to talk.

"It's just that Gwen's gone missing too," he said.

"Oh . . . !" She let out a long breath, and pressed a hand to her heart as if that might help to steady it, but an odd look of relief appeared on her face. "Well, that at least makes sense, doesn't it? It's a bit shattering, but it does explain . . . I mean, if the two of them were planning to go away together, it's natural he might not want to leave a message about it. But he's all right, nothing awful has happened to him, and we'll hear from him as soon as they've made up their minds what to do. Of course I'm sorry about it, because for one thing I suppose that Nicholas—well, if he knew what they were planning, he might have gone out of his mind, mightn't he, and done that fearful thing with the bomb? But for the moment anyway we needn't worry about Jonathan."

"It isn't quite as simple as that," Colin said.

She had poured herself out another cup of coffee, and now sat down again.

"What isn't?" she asked.

"It's just that Gwen doesn't seem to have taken a suitcase or any clothes away with her," Colin said. "She took her handbag, and Nicholas thinks she'd a fair amount of money in it, as she cashed a cheque when they were in Rockford, meeting Lyn. But if she and Jonathan were going away together, wouldn't she have taken some clothes?"

"Who says she hasn't?" Dorothea asked.

Colin looked puzzled. "I'm not sure. It was Nicholas who told me."

"Look, if I were suddenly to disappear," she said, "and I took half my clothes away with me, would you be able to tell the police just what I'd taken when you reported me missing? Think it over. This is mid-winter, and I suppose she and Jonathan are heading for somewhere lovely in the sun, and she's got all her summer clothes out of the wardrobe. Do you think Nicholas is really able to say what she's taken?"

Colin stared thoughtfully in front of him.

"I see what you mean. Perhaps not. But if it was you who'd gone, I'd remember that black and white spotted dress of yours. I'd be able to tell the police whether or not you'd left that behind. And I might notice it if a suitcase was missing."

"Has she taken her passport?" Andrew asked.

He realised that it must sound as if he had passports on the brain, but they did seem to him to be more significant at the moment than black and white spotted dresses or even suitcases. He himself would notice if a suitcase of his own were missing, but he knew that a lot of people accumulate them in some attic when they have become too battered for use, and that after two or three years it would become impossible for them to say if one was missing.

"I didn't think of asking," Colin said.

"And they hadn't thought of looking for it?"

"I suppose not, or they'd have mentioned it, wouldn't they?"

"But when did she vanish?" Dorothea demanded. "This morning?"

"No, that's a bit complicated too," Colin said. "Nicholas went to bed quite early yesterday evening because he'd been feeling pretty bad all day, and Gwen gave him a sleeping pill and he was sound asleep by eleven or half past. He didn't wake up at all till about eight in the morning, and then he saw that Gwen's bed hadn't been slept in." He paused. "You understand, I'm only repeating what he told me."

"Have you any doubts of it then?" Andrew asked.

"Not really. No, I'm sure it was the truth as far as he knew it, but we can't be sure, can we, just how many pills Gwen gave him. He admitted that if he takes one, he always has it crushed up because he's no good at swallowing. But I know I don't really want to believe him. And Lyn Goddard said she'd heard Gwen go up to her room around midnight. She'd gone up earlier herself, but hadn't gone to sleep. And she didn't hear Gwen come down again, but that's what she must have done."

"Did you tell them that Jonathan's missing?" Andrew asked.

"Yes, I had to, hadn't I? It's all too obvious what happened. She may or may not have packed a suitcase, then taken her handbag with what money she had in it, met Jonathan in the lane and gone off with him. And if I'd said nothing about Jonathan, Nicholas might have called the police to help find Gwen, but now he won't, or not for the moment, so we've a little time to think out what we ought to do."

"I'm not sure if you know that Jonathan met Gwen in The Running Man yesterday evening after she got back from London," Andrew said, seeing no further virtue in discretion. "I believe he told you he was going to have a drink with a friend. Well, the friend was Gwen. I saw Jonathan getting out of her car as I was leaving the Deardens' after handing over the manuscript, and when I caught up with him in the garden we talked about what he'd been doing."

"So that's when they planned it." Dorothea sounded close to tears, but she drank some more coffee and made an effort to steady her voice. "If only he'd told us what they were going to do. We wouldn't have tried to stop them. We haven't been happy about the relationship between them, but we never dreamt of interfering. I mean, that sort of thing goes on all the time, one just has to accept that. But he might have left us a message or something."

Colin stood up abruptly. For once he had lost his look of placid competence. He looked depressed and defeated.

"I'm going to get on with some work," he said. "Sitting here trying to persuade ourselves we can sort out the problem by going on and on talking about it isn't going to get us anywhere. See you later."

"Oh, Colin, please—!" Dorothea began and stopped.

He paused in the doorway. "What is it?"

"No, go on," she said. "You're quite right, talking doesn't help. Only everything seems so awful. I think I'll go and rake up those dead leaves on the lawn that ought to have been cleared up weeks ago and make a bonfire— Oh my God, no, how could I think of that? A fire! But I'll rake them up anyway and put them on the compost heap."

She fetched a jacket from a peg in the hall, kicked off her slippers and struggled into Wellingtons, put on gardening gloves and went out by the back door. Colin went upstairs and after a few minutes Andrew heard the clicking of his typewriter.

As the things that had been used for breakfast were still on the table, Andrew thought he might as well wash them up. When he had done that, he set out to visit Mrs. Cambrey.

The bungalow, Elsinore, was a small, square white building with a red tiled roof, a bright blue front door and lacey nylon curtains in all the windows. When Andrew rang the bell he heard musical chimes inside and thought how desperately he would come to hate their melody if he had anything of the sort at his own door. A moment after he had rung he heard swift footsteps approaching the door, and it was opened.

A small, plump, friendly-looking woman stood there. She was about forty, he thought, had an abundance of light brown curls clustering around her round pink face, full cheeks and a neat little mouth with slightly protruding lips. She wore glasses with very pale pink rims over her soft brown eyes, a pale pink nylon overall over a dark dress, and pink bedroom slippers with furry trimmings. She began to greet him, with a surprisingly warm smile that showed sparkling teeth, then changed her mind abruptly and said, "Sorry, I thought you were the paper boy. I was going to give him something. But of course he won't be coming on Boxing Day, will he? What can I do for you?"

"Mrs. Cambrey?" Andrew asked.

"Yes," she said.

"My name's Basnett," he said. "I'm a friend of Mr. and Mrs. Cahill's. I've been spending Christmas with them and it happens—"

"Christmas!" she shrieked at him before he could say any more. "In Stillmore Lane! Oh, you poor man, what a time you must have had. You were there, I suppose when—when that—that thing went off."

"Yes, I was, as a matter of fact," he said, "and it's because of something that in a way has something to do with that that I've come to see you. If you've a few minutes to spare—"

"Me!" she broke in again. She was the sort of woman, he guessed, who very seldom let anyone else finish a sentence. "What information could I possibly have? Or Norman either. We were both in The Running Man when it happened and we heard it and someone said, 'That's thunder,' and I said— But what am I doing, leaving you here? Come in, I know I can't help you, but come in."

Her eyes were alight with curiosity. If Andrew had agreed with her just then that she would not be able to help him, and turned to leave, he would have found it very difficult to get away.

She took him into a small, square room furnished with a three-piece suite covered in some kind of very shiny bright blue synthetic velvet, a coffee table of black glass with metal legs, one or two other odd tables of the same kind and a television with a bowl of plastic flowers standing on it. There was a tiled fireplace with a fire laid very neatly in the grate, but not lit. It was depressingly cold, but she did not seem to feel this herself.

"You'll have a cup of tea," she stated as she invited him to sit in one of the gleaming velvet chairs.

"No, thank you, it's very kind of you, but I've only just had breakfast," he said. "But I might ask you—"

"As I was saying," she interrupted once more, " 'No,' I said, 'it isn't thunder, it's a bomb,' and we all started laughing. Imagine that! Laughing like mad as if I'd made the best joke in the world. A bomb in Upper Cullonden! And then later on hearing what had happened I felt terrible, I promise you. Of course we'd all had a few drinks and I didn't mean anything, but all the same, to have that on my mind for the rest of my life! But that isn't why you came to see me, is it, because there are lots of people can say Norman and I were there most of the evening and the police have been all round the village, asking questions, and I even told them how I said, 'No, that isn't thunder.' "

As she paused momentarily for breath Andrew adroitly slid in a few words.

"I believe you typed a manuscript for Sir Lucas Dearden."

"That's right, I did," she said, hurriedly recuperating from her brief silence. "I often do odd jobs for people. I used to be a secretary until I married, and sometimes I get bored, just housekeeping and all that, and there's the money too, of course. Sir Lucas paid pretty well, though he was a bit fussy about mistakes. He was what you call a perfectionist. He wanted everything to be perfect. Not that I ever make many mistakes, but now and then the odd one gets in, how could you expect anything else, but I think he got as clean a copy from me as he'd have got from anyone. If you do a job at all, it's worth doing well, that's what I believe, and if he recommended me to you, or you know of someone who wants something done—"

"No." Andrew interrupted her by slightly raising his voice in a manner which in the past had often silenced troublesome students. "I want to ask you if you happened to notice if page 96 was missing from his manuscript."

Her alternative to loquacity was a deep and thoughtful withdrawal into herself. She sat looking at one hand, which she held up before her as if to examine the pink polish on its nails.

"Well, now that you mention it," she began, then paused.

"Yes?" he prompted her.

"It was kind of strange, though I never thought much about it, but if it's important . . . Is it important?"

"I won't know that till you tell me what was strange," he answered.

"It was only that a week or so after I'd got started on the job—you understand, I only work at odd times when I've time to spare, so I may be slower than some people—well, I'd hardly got started on it when Sir Lucas turned up here and said he'd been having second thoughts about something he'd written and he wanted to change it. So I take out the manuscript and I give it to him and he turns to page—what did you say it was, 96?—and he just rips it out. I say, 'But look, Sir Lucas, I've typed that already, do you want me to do it again?' And he says yes, please, and of course he'll pay me extra. So that was how it was. He tore the page out and crumpled it up and dropped it in the fire and said he was sorry to give trouble, but he looked at the manuscript and gave a kind of laugh and said, 'It reads pretty well as it is, doesn't it? I needn't write anything different.' So I typed the last few pages I'd done over again and sure enough, except that I had to change the numbers of the pages, it was all just as I'd done it before."

"Then you'd already typed that page he tore out," Andrew said. "Can you remember anything about it?"

"Not very much. I didn't see really why he wanted to tear it out, but he said it was too personal and it said something that might upset his daughter and son-in-law. I couldn't see that myself. It was only a mention that she'd got engaged to a young man whose name I'm sorry I forget, but you could tell from the way he wrote about him that Sir Lucas didn't think much of him. The man was an actor or something, I think, and seemed to be mainly out of work, then he was killed in a car crash and right away she goes and gets engaged to Mr. Haslam, who's got plenty of money and a senior job in some firm he works for, and Sir Lucas is a bit afraid she's doing it on the rebound and that it won't work out, specially as this second man is a good bit older than she is. But then it all turns out very well because this Mr. Haslam is a really good sort of chap and crazy about her. And that's all, so far as I remember it."

"Thank you," Andrew said, "that's very interesting. Am I right that it's your impression that he only wanted to cut out what was on that page because it made a little too much of a purely personal event?"

"That's it," she said. "That's it exactly."

"Most of the book is pretty impersonal, isn't it?"

"Well, that's what I thought myself, I mean, I didn't find it interesting. But I don't claim to be a judge. I know Sir Lucas was a very clever man and perhaps there are people who like to read that sort of thing. And he paid me promptly and said I'd done a very nice piece of work. I wish all my clients were as thoughtful. I mean, one does want to be appreciated."

"Of course. But there was really nothing else on that missing page but the reference to his daughter's former engagement?"

She gave a slow, thoughtful shake of her head, once more appearing to have withdrawn deeply into herself. She frowned a little, as if she were trying to capture some memory.

"Now you mention it . . ." she said at length.

"Yes?" Andrew said.

"I don't remember it exactly, it was only a line or so, but there was some mention of Miss Dearden having been engaged to someone before the actor chap. I don't think it said who it was, but only that she'd got engaged when she was much too young to think of marriage and it was lucky it got broken off. I think Sir Lucas was very relieved when he saw her safely married to Mr. Haslam. But I wonder if Mr. Haslam knew about any of that, and if it was perhaps because he didn't that Sir Lucas felt he ought to tear out the page. After all, what does being engaged mean nowadays? You can easily say you've got a boy-friend or what have you, and it may mean anything. All this getting engaged—does it sound at all queer to you?"

"I don't think so," Andrew said. "It's a habit some people get into. I had an aunt who got engaged nineteen times."

"Ah yes, but that was long ago, wasn't it? Things are different now."

"That's true." Yet under the surface how different were they, he asked himself. His Aunt Madge had been a very beautiful woman who had attracted men round her like the proverbial flies round a honey-pot, had eventually got married, divorced, remarried and then had died in childbirth. That last perhaps would not have happened now. Some antibiotics might have saved her. But the life that she had lived had not been so different from the life of the young and the beautiful nowadays. He had been told that Erica Haslam was beautiful. He thought that he would question Nicholas about her, then he remembered that Nicholas's wife had gone missing that day and that he was unlikely to be much interested in a sister.

On his walk back to the Cahills' house Andrew saw that the portion of the lane that had been roped off was now clear. He had not noticed it when he set out. Letting himself into the house, he heard voices in the sitting-room. They were men's voices. One was Colin's, but the other was unfamiliar.

For a moment Andrew thought that it belonged to Detective Inspector Roland, and that after all Nicholas had reported the disappearance of his wife to the police, and that Jonathan's disappearance not unnaturally had been linked to it and that that was why they were here. But it was not Roland in the room. It was a man whom Andrew had not seen before.

Colin introduced them to one another.

"This is Henry Haslam, Andrew. Professor Basnett, Henry."

Henry Haslam was standing in front of the fireplace. He held out a hand. He was a large, powerful-looking man with heavy features in a ruddy, almost unwrinkled face, but with a considerable paunch that made him look older than he probably was. What hair he had was grey, and there was not a great deal of it. He had straight eyebrows that almost met above his short, thick nose and slightly protuberant eyes. His dark brown worsted suit was very well cut; his shoes looked expensive. There was an air of opulence about him that Andrew recognised at once, though he would have found it difficult to say why he did so. It was not purely the result of the suit and the shoes, but something to do with the man's air of physical confidence, of being a man who had always eaten and drunk well, and had control of others.

"I've often heard about you, Professor," Henry Haslam said. "Colin and I are old friends. My wife and I often come down here and of course we met long ago. But it's never been for an occasion like this."

"How is your wife?" Andrew asked. "I've heard about her accident."

"She's as well as can be expected," Haslam said. "Doing pretty well, actually. She's very tough. And the hospital's a good one. She'll soon be over the worst." His voice was deep and resonant, with an accent that had been acquired at one of the better public schools. "I've only come down for the day, or anyway, that's what I intended, but finding the state Nicholas is in I can't help wondering if I ought to stay longer. But perhaps I might come back tomorrow. I haven't brought any clothes with me, so staying wouldn't be too easy. And the drive takes only about an hour and a half—less today, because of course being Boxing Day there wasn't much traffic. But even tomorrow when everyone's going home I could get here quite early. Only I'm not sure if it's necessary. That girl Lyn Goddard seems to have everything under control."

"Is there still no news of Gwen?" Andrew asked.

"No," Colin said.

"Or of Jonathan?"

"No."

"What a thing for them to have done!" Haslam exclaimed. "Not that I'm altogether surprised. I've known for some time that Nicholas and Gwen weren't really hitting it off, but I never connected her with Jonathan, or with anyone else for that matter. Forgive me, Dorothea, I know it's painful for you to talk about it, but it's best to face it. They've chosen this extraordinary time to disappear together and it makes one wonder . . . I don't mean I'm wondering if either of them had anything to do with the bomb, but I can't help thinking how wrong one can be about people, even people one thinks one knows well. You know, I'm very sorry for Nicholas, because I believe some people are suspicious of him, but of course there's no possible doubt it was that man Waterman who did it. And all my fault too."

"Why do you say that, Henry?" Dorothea asked. As usual she was on the sofa with her feet up. "How can you have had anything to do with it?"

Haslam waved one of his thick hands in the air in a gesture that might have been an apology.

"My crass stupidity," he said. "Waterman rang me up just a short time after I'd got Erica settled in St. Raphael's and got home, and he asked me when I thought he could see Lucas. I thought the man was in London, that was the mistake I made. I didn't trouble to ask him where he was ringing from, and I said he couldn't see Lucas because he'd gone home."

"So Nicholas was wrong about that," Colin said. "He told the police he was sure you wouldn't have said anything of the sort because you'd have remembered the business of the threats Waterman shouted from the dock."

"I did, I did," Haslam said, "and that's precisely why I said Lucas had gone home. I thought I was getting rid of Waterman, when in fact I was doing just the reverse. But I was in a pretty shattered state after Erica's accident and not thinking too clearly. All the same I blame myself very seriously. I only hope the police have got the man."

"He's denied having been in touch with you," Colin said.

"Well, he's lying. I'm going into Rockford to see the police directly. But I wanted to see you before I went because I wanted to find out if you'd mind if I said something about Gwen and Jonathan having gone off together, or if you'd sooner I said nothing about it."

Colin turned to Andrew.

"What do you think?" he asked. "We won't be able to keep the thing hidden for long."

"No, no!" Dorothea cried. "It's got nothing to do with what happened to Lucas. It's an altogether private matter. Please don't say anything about it, Henry."

"But what do you think about it, Andrew?" Colin repeated.

Andrew felt his usual deep reluctance to give advice. He had sat down in a low easy chair, and this made the heavy figure of Henry Haslam seem to tower above him. Yet Andrew felt some pity for him, because powerful and sure of himself as he appeared, his distress at what he had done seemed genuine.

"I don't really see why the subject need come up," Andrew said. "Of course if Roland asks Mr. Haslam about it, the only thing to do will be to tell the truth. But you can easily explain later why you didn't say anything about it before. That is, that you felt it was a private matter and you were still waiting, hoping to hear from Jonathan or Gwen."

"And that's just what we're doing," Dorothea said, "so please say nothing about it, Henry, unless they ask you directly, when I agree you must tell the truth. Andrew, did you see that woman this morning, that Mrs. Cambrey?"

"Yes," he said.

"And had she anything of interest to say about that missing page?"

Everything that she had had to say about it concerned Henry Haslam's wife, and Andrew did not know how much the man might know about it.

"I'm not sure," he said.

"Who's Mrs. Cambrey?" Haslam asked. "Is she someone involved in all this?"

"She's just a woman who typed Lucas's memoirs," Dorothea said. "I suppose there was nothing about Waterman on that page 96, was there, Andrew?"

"Not according to her," he answered.

"I wonder where he is now?" she said. "Perhaps the police have taken him in for questioning."

"Or perhaps he's slipped through their fingers and is in France or somewhere by now," Colin suggested.

"Well, I must go and tell them my share of things," Haslam said. "I find it difficult to understand now how I could have been such a fool, but I was, and the sooner they know about it, the better. Good-bye, Professor. I've always hoped to meet you sometime, after hearing Colin and Dorothea talk about you, but not like this. Another time, perhaps."

He and Colin left the room together.

Dorothea swung her feet down from the sofa and leant tensely forward, gazing at Andrew.

"What did that woman really say?" she asked.

"Mrs. Cambrey? Not much," he replied. "She remembered the missing page. Dearden came to see her and tore it out after she'd typed it, and she had to do some of the job over again. His reasons appear to have been that he felt it was too personal. It was simply about Mrs. Haslam having been engaged twice before she married Haslam. One of her fiancés was apparently killed in a car accident. I don't know anything about the other."

"Oh, everyone knew about that!" Dorothea exclaimed. "She had an affair with a married man which she flaunted everywhere. She told us all he was going to have a divorce and marry her. Then he decided not to have the divorce but to stick to his wife, and the two of them went off together, I believe to New Zealand."

"And does Haslam know all about that?"

"Oh yes, it was a very public thing. Poor kid, I think she was only about nineteen at the time and didn't know anything about the disadvantages of being 'the other woman.' "

"So page 96 really tells us nothing—" Andrew broke off as the telephone rang.

Dorothea leapt towards it almost as if she had known it would ring at that moment.

"Yes," she said excitedly, "yes, of course it's me. But where are you, darling? . . . *Heathrow!* You can't mean it . . . But why? . . . Where are you going? . . . No, isn't she with you? . . . She isn't? But she must be. I mean, where is she if she isn't with you? . . . No, Jonathan, she's disappeared too and of course we all thought you were together . . . But of course that's what we thought. It's what Nicholas thinks too. Poor man, he's going nearly mad with worry, but if she isn't with you . . . Oh, Jonathan, please come home at once, it's the only thing for you to do . . . Yes, do that, we'll expect you in about an hour, it won't take you much more than that to get here. And I'm so sorry, darling, if things have gone wrong for you, but I just don't know anything about what's happened except that she's missing . . . All right then, we won't say anything to Nicholas until you get back, but it might be a case for the police . . . Yes, yes, we'll wait."

She drew a deep breath as she put the telephone down. For

a moment she stood staring blankly at the wall before her, then she turned to Andrew.

"He's been at Heathrow all night and he's been expecting Gwen to join him," she said. "But she hasn't come. I think that's something to be thankful for. But what can possibly have happened to her?"

SEVEN

IT WAS A LITTLE OVER an hour later that Jonathan returned. Dorothea, as always, seemed more concerned about providing him with lunch than in hearing why he had left for Heathrow the night before without leaving any message behind. She had given Colin and Andrew a lunch of omelettes and coffee and was anxious to do the same for Jonathan, but he rejected it with some impatience, saying that he had just had a good breakfast at Heathrow and now only wanted a drink. It was whisky that he wanted, which was unusual for him. His face, which normally looked so healthy, had a pallid, almost withered look. His eyes were red-veined with fatigue.

"Now what's all this about Gwen?" he asked. He had dropped into a chair in the sitting-room and had drunk about half of his whisky quickly, as if he were relying on it to clear his mind. "She can't really have disappeared."

"That's what we said about you when we found you'd gone missing," Dorothea said. "We thought perhaps you might just have driven off by yourself for a time to think quietly about what you ought to do. If it hadn't been for your passport being missing . . . But we never really hunted for it. I thought perhaps you'd just moved it to a different drawer or something. Where were you meaning to go, Jonathan?"

"Does it matter?" he said. "I don't really know."

"You don't know!" she exclaimed. "You mean you went to Heathrow and you didn't even know where you were going?"

"That's just about it," he said. "We'd have seen what tickets were available. I was rather hoping we'd get to Monte Carlo or somewhere like that. Gwen had quite a bit of money available, so she said, and I'd my credit card. We'd probably have taken a stand-by flight to somewhere or other. It didn't seem to me to matter much where we ended up once she'd at last agreed to come with me, as I thought she had. Oh God, I'm tired. Have we got to go on talking about it?"

"I thought you wanted to know what had happened to her," Colin said.

"And you don't know," Jonathan replied. "What I'd like is to get out of my clothes and have a bath and go to bed."

"When did you see her last?" Colin asked.

Jonathan gave a deep yawn.

"Yesterday evening," he said. "In The Running Man. She phoned me from there after she'd got back from seeing Erica and said she wanted to see me. And as you know, I told you I was going there to have a drink with a friend. And I thought she wanted to see me to make some final arrangements about our leaving. We'd decided days ago—before Christmas, before the bomb—that we'd leave together on Boxing Day and go to the South of France, and once we were there we'd really think about the future. I thought we ought simply to tell Nicholas how things were and leave openly, but she seemed to be scared of doing that, though she never quite explained why. Then when I met her at The Running Man she told me that she wanted to call the whole thing off."

"For good, or just temporarily, till the shock of the bomb had worn off a little?" Colin enquired.

"I don't think she knew herself," Jonathan said.

"But you persuaded her to go ahead with your plan."

"Yes."

"There are some things about it I don't understand," Andrew said. "Why didn't you pick her up at her gate and take her to Heathrow in your car?"

"Because we weren't sure when she'd be able to get out," Jonathan said. "Our idea was that she'd wait till she was sure Nicholas was asleep—she was going to give him a couple of sleeping pills—then she'd slip out. But we didn't know when that would be, and if I'd been in my car, waiting perhaps for quite a long time somewhere in the lane, someone might have seen it and thought it was a bit queer my just waiting there. If the police had been around, for instance, they might actually have stopped us getting away. So we thought it'd be best if I simply drove off to Heathrow on my own and she'd follow me in her car when she could safely get away. And I got to Heathrow and I waited and I waited . . ." He finished his whisky and gave another exhausted yawn. "Well, that's about all. I kept on hoping, and it wasn't until about halfway through this morning that I admitted to myself she simply wasn't coming. Until then I kept telling myself she hadn't been able to get away in the night because Nicholas hadn't gone to sleep or something. But in the morning she could easily have taken her car, saying she was going on some errand, then actually driven off to join me. But in the end I understood she'd simply agreed to all our plans the evening before as a way of keeping me quiet and getting rid of me. She never meant to come."

"Except that now she's missing," Colin said, "so she went somewhere."

"What about her car?" Jonathan asked. "Is that missing too?"

"No," Colin said, "and nor are any of her clothes or a suitcase, or so Nicholas says. Dorothea isn't inclined to believe him."

"That isn't true," Dorothea said. "I only feel it isn't absolutely certain that he'd know if she'd taken anything with her. But I'm sure he's right when he says her handbag's missing. He says she took that away with her."

"So if she wasn't carrying anything like a suitcase, she could easily have walked away," Jonathan said. He frowned thoughtfully. "If she'd left in the early morning, not in the night, she could have caught a bus into Rockford, then she could have taken a train to London, and from there . . . D'you know, I believe I ought to have gone on waiting at Heathrow. She could have gone there from Victoria, but it would have taken her till later in the morning to do it. Yes, honestly I believe that's what she may have done! Nicholas didn't go to sleep, or she wasn't sure that he did, and so she simply slipped away very quietly out of the house without bothering about a suitcase, and didn't take the car because opening up the garage and so on might have disturbed him, and set off on foot." He sprang to his feet. "Look, I've got to get back to Heathrow as quickly as I can."

"Jonathan darling, sit down," Dorothea said. "Or go and have that bath you want and some sleep. She isn't waiting for you at Heathrow. If she really went there in the way you think, she'll have realised when she got there and couldn't find you that you'd given her up and gone home. So she'll either phone you here or she'll come here herself. Or what I think is more probable is that she didn't go to Heathrow at all, but went somewhere to escape from both you and Nicholas and think things out in peace. And if that sounds cruel to you, I'm sorry, but I can understand how she may have felt that she'd got to do something of the sort. You say she's scared of Nicholas, and for all we know she's scared of you too. I think she's a person who's always been scared of a lot of things."

"But where could she go if she hasn't got a suitcase?" Jonathan asked. "Hotels don't exactly make you welcome if you haven't any luggage."

"Has she any special friends or relations she might have gone to?" Colin asked.

"Not that I know of," Jonathan said. "I know her parents are dead."

"A place she might have gone to," Dorothea said, "if she got to London, is the Haslams' flat. I believe Henry was there for the night, but he said he was going to come back here in the morning, so if she didn't get there too early she'd have had the place to herself."

"But how would she have got in?"

"Didn't she go to see Erica in the hospital yesterday, and mightn't she have told Erica the whole story, and mightn't Erica actually have suggested she should go to the flat to hide for a little while, and given her her own key? You know I think that might be the answer to the whole problem. You see, she could even borrow Erica's clothes."

Jonathan gave his mother a wondering look, as he sometimes did when he thought she was talking sense.

"Then what I've got to do is to telephone the Haslams' flat," he said. "Have you got their number?"

"No," Dorothea said, "but I can get it in a moment from the Deardens."

"I'd stick to Directory Enquiries," Colin said. "If Nicholas answers he's liable to be specially anxious to get you to help him trace his wife, which perhaps you don't yet want to do."

"If I were you, I wouldn't phone at all," Andrew said. "She seems to have made it evident that she wants to be left in peace."

But Jonathan was not inclined to follow this advice. He dialled Directory Enquiries, asking for the Haslams' number, and afterwards dialled the number that he was given. He held the telephone to his ear for a long time while the ringing tone went on and on. Then at last he put the telephone down with a slam and without a word went out of the room.

"So I was wrong," Dorothea said. "She isn't there."

"Or she's gone out, or knowing that it was probably Jonathan ringing, didn't choose to answer," Colin said.

"And now what are we going to do?" she asked. "Oh, I've begun to hate that woman. I don't believe Jonathan's ever meant anything to her and she doesn't care how much he gets hurt."

"I think the first thing we've got to do is tell Nicholas that Jonathan has come home and that Gwen isn't with him," Colin said. "I'll go round right away. It might be a good idea if you come too. You may be able to get Lyn to talk to you."

Dorothea nodded and went to fetch a coat. The two of them left the house together.

Andrew decided to indulge himself for once in a short sleep and sat down in a chair near to the electric fire. But sleep did not come. He felt drowsy enough, but failed to slip away into complete unconsciousness. After a little while rhymes took over in his brain.

> Heap on more wood!—the wind is chill,
> But let it whistle as it will,
> We'll keep our Christmas merry still . . .

It was maddening, but there was one thing for which he was thankful. Christmas was over. There was holly still along the tops of the pictures, and there were Christmas cards looking gay on the tree-branch in its pot of earth, but the challenge to be merry had gone. With luck, he thought, he might never again feel any obligation to be merry at Christmas. Next year he might just lay in a good supply of frozen food, lock and bolt the door against the world, leave the telephone unanswered and wait until Christmas and New Year were safely past before emerging. For any festivity, any dinner with friends, any party however pleasant, would only remind him of the tragedy of Upper Cullonden and leave him with an ache in his heart.

Colin and Dorothea were really very dear friends, and he could not help sharing in the pain that they were suffering, all of which was connected, of course, with the folly of their son. If he had not started a love-affair with that woman next door, if he had not chosen the most preposterous of times to try to elope with her, if the bomb in the lane had not so very probably been meant for him, Christmas might have been no worse than most Christmases were for childless people—a time, that was to say, of over-eating, often followed by indigestion; of drinking more than usual, which it was true was a help; and a slightly futile attempt to recapture some of the joys of childhood.

" 'Heap on more wood!'—" No, he did not intend to let those lines occupy his mind. The best way to prevent that, he knew, was to think of some other lines. But when he tried to do this, all that came to him were some ridiculous words.

> I gotta phone,
> You gotta phone,
> All God's chilluns got phones,
> When I get to Heaven goin' to phone all my friends,
> Goin' to ring up all over God's Heaven . . .

He sat up with a start. Had he actually been asleep for a little while? Telephones, of course, were on his mind because the question of who could have telephoned whom seemed to be a central matter in the disaster here. Henry Haslam admitted that he had had a call from Thomas Waterman on the day of the bombing.

Was that important?

Lyn Goddard insisted that no one had called the Deardens on that day.

Was that true?

Gwen Dearden had called Jonathan, asking him to meet her at The Running Man, and there, according to him, she had promised to meet him later at Heathrow.

Was that really what she had done?

Jonathan had called Dorothea from Heathrow to say that Gwen had never arrived. Then what had happened to her? She had not answered when Jonathan telephoned the Haslams' flat, but had she been there? Who could tell? Not the telephone itself. It occurred to Andrew that life must really have been far simpler before the fearful thing was invented. Fearful because few things could produce such a sense of nervous frustration as a call that ought to have been made but was not, or one that simply went unanswered.

Andrew began to think about Gwen. He had never before given her much thought. She was nice-looking, even charming, courteous and sufficiently intelligent, or so she had always seemed to him; but what was there about her to make a young man like Jonathan, who was attractive enough himself to have a fairly wide choice open to him among women, fall so fatally in love with her? For fatal perhaps it had been. If it had been Nicholas who planted the bomb, and jealousy had been his motive . . .

But that would mean that he too was passionately devoted to her, no doubt with a slightly insane sort of love, but one which nevertheless was powerful enough to drive him to an act of incredible horror. What was there about her to make it even possible to think of such things? Under her quiet exterior there must be a great wealth of emotion, of passion, of tenderness, the possession of which perhaps she herself did not fully understand. At all events, she had not wanted to make use of them. Challenged, she had fled. She had escaped, gone into hiding, rejected all that was offered to her. She was more than a little neurotic, Andrew was inclined to think, a person who took refuge in hysteria as soon as she was shocked or frightened. But many very neurotic people have great charm . . .

Andrew started, for the door had suddenly opened; Jonathan came in.

"Are they still over there?" he asked, giving a nod vaguely in the direction of the Deardens' house.

"So far as I know," Andrew answered.

Jonathan sat down on the sofa where his mother normally sat. Almost as if he were imitating her, he put his feet up, and leaning back against the cushions, folded his hands under his head and crossed his ankles. Andrew considered him with detachment. He was certainly good-looking, with more suggestion of strength about him than there was about Nicholas, which was not only because of his youth. Rather, Andrew thought, it was in spite of his youth. There was an air of promise about him, of qualities yet to develop. If Gwen had stuck to the plan that she and Jonathan were said to have made in The Running Man, Andrew would not have found it surprising.

"I've made up my mind, I'm going to move into Rockford," Jonathan said.

"That may be a good idea," Andrew said.

"Of course I can't do it at once," Jonathan went on. "I'll have to wait until things have calmed down. Then I think I'll go into lodgings for a bit, then look for a flat. There's just one problem."

"Yes?"

"I don't want them to feel hurt at my moving out. Do you think they will?"

"Not very seriously. As a matter of fact, it may be a bit of a relief to them."

"Because of getting me away from Gwen? That's partly why I want to go, of course. I don't think she'll come back till I go."

"You think she will come back?"

"Why not?"

"Will Nicholas want her back?"

"No doubt about it. After what he's done to keep her . . ."

No!" Jonathan raised a hand to stop Andrew speaking. "I know what you're going to say. And of course I realise we haven't the least certainty he did it, but unless they find the man who did, she'll go on having that little doubt at the back of her mind and she won't stay with him."

"Rockford isn't very far away," Andrew said. "You could still see her."

"I'll only do that if she comes looking for me." There was a sudden sternness on Jonathan's face, which gave him the air that he sometimes had of being older than he was. "But what I wanted to ask you, Andrew, is will you tell Mum for me what I mean to do, and if she's upset, try to convince her that it's the best thing for all of us."

"As I said, I don't think she'll be too much upset," Andrew said. "She's had a feeling of guilt about your living here, in case it's because she's been too possessive. She's read all the right books about that sort of thing."

"All the same, it's what she is, you know. You can show a sort of possessiveness by holding back and letting it be seen how much that hurts you. I think I did that with Gwen."

"I didn't know there was much holding back on your part."

"Oh yes, there was!"

"Yet you stayed on here, just to be near her."

Jonathan gave a short little bark of laughter. "All right, I did, and you don't approve of it. And you're quite right, it's ended in ruin for all of us. But what do you think I ought to have done? Give her up, I suppose."

"I didn't say that."

"But honestly, what do you think I ought to have done?"

"I haven't any idea," Andrew answered, "except that at the moment I feel you're putting on an act of some sort. I'm not sure if you're just trying to convince me that you're giving Gwen up when you've no intention of doing so, or if you're really trying to convince yourself about it. But something doesn't ring quite true."

"Do you care much which it is?"

"Why should I?"

"Because for one thing you're very attached to my parents, and if you couldn't care less what happens to me, you do care about them. So if my walking out now, or as soon as I can get away, is going to hurt them, it'll worry you. Perhaps not very much. You're always careful not to get too involved with other people, but you'll blame me for it."

"You seem to want me to blame you for something."

Jonathan swung his feet down abruptly and sat facing Andrew, holding his head in his hands.

"Oh, Andrew, I don't. It's just that I'm in such a mess. Everything's such a mess. Really I want you to tell me you don't blame me."

Andrew thought over his answer for a moment before he said, "Let's leave it at that. You aren't a child anymore. You've got to sort those things out for yourself."

Jonathan closed his eyes for an instant, then opened them and stared at the carpet at his feet.

"You're right, of course. I'm sorry I bothered you."

As he said it Andrew heard the front door open and close, and Colin and Dorothea came into the room.

Colin had an arm round Dorothea, as if in some way he were trying to protect her. They stood looking rather vacantly at Andrew and Jonathan, but almost at once Dorothea shot off to the kitchen to get tea. There were no cucumber sandwiches that afternoon, but only some slightly stale biscuits. When Andrew asked if there was any news of Gwen, Colin replied that there was not. He added that when he had told Nicholas of Jonathan's waiting for her at Heathrow, Nicholas had decided to call the police and report that she was missing. He believed that, after the explosion of the bomb and seeing what she had of her father-in-law's body in the burning car in the lane, she might be suffering so severely from shock that she was experiencing an attack of amnesia and perhaps might be wandering somewhere now, alone and lost.

Colin and Dorothea had not attempted to dissuade him from telling this to the police, but had left before they arrived. All the time that Colin was talking Jonathan sat as he had been when they came in, staring down at the carpet with his elbows on his knees and his head in his hands.

When Dorothea wheeled the tea-trolley into the room he raised his head and said, "They'll be coming here any time now, won't they?"

"I expect so," Colin said.

"And they'll want to question me. And d'you know what I'd like to do? I'd like to get into my car and drive off fast. I don't know where. Anywhere. Only there'd be no point in doing it really, because they'd catch up with me sooner or later." Jonathan accepted the cup of tea that his mother held out to him and looked up at her with a trace of a smile. "It's all right, Mum, I don't really mean to do it. I'm going to wait here like a good boy and answer everything they ask me. But I don't believe in the amnesia theory. I think Gwen knew only too well what she was doing."

"Henry's still over there," Colin said. "After all he didn't go home yesterday evening. Nicholas lent him a pair of Lucas's pyjamas and Lucas's razor this morning, and just what they did about a toothbrush I don't know. Perhaps they had a spare in the house."

"I wonder why he stayed," Jonathan said.

"I think he felt it might make things easier for Nicholas and Lyn," Dorothea said. "You know what Henry's like. Conventional to the limit. He probably felt there'd be some impropriety about leaving them there alone together and that it was his duty to stay."

"If anyone felt that, Lyn could have come here, couldn't she?" Jonathan said.

"Anyway, she didn't," Colin replied with an abruptness that showed how much his nerves were on edge. He seemed to avoid looking at Jonathan, as if by doing that he could avoid the thought that it was at least to some extent Jonathan's doing that Gwen had vanished.

The police did not arrive until a little after five o'clock. Detective Inspector Roland's square face with the heavy-lidded eyes had a look of grimness about it which Andrew noticed, wondering why he had not specially done so before. Then he thought that perhaps he had been aware of it from the first but had preferred not to think that Roland had any strong feelings, other than purely professional ones, about the case on which he was engaged. But now it seemed to Andrew the man was angry. Perhaps only angry because he was being kept from going home for his tea, or else because he felt bewildered and unsure of himself and did not like the condition. Sergeant Porter had his usual look of being somehow pleasantly surprised at finding himself in such agreeable company.

Dorothea immediately offered the two detectives tea, but Roland refused it for both of them with only the merest shake of his head.

"If you don't mind, I'd like to ask Mr. Jonathan Cahill one or two questions," he said and in his usual way added, "Nothing important probably, but he may be able to help us." He sat down in the chair that Colin had offered him, but his eyes were steadily on Jonathan. "I believe you had planned to go abroad with Mrs. Dearden."

"So I thought," Jonathan said.

"When did you decide to do this?" Roland asked.

"Yesterday evening."

"You mean you hadn't thought of doing it before that?"

"Yes, of course we had. We'd been thinking of it for months. But there always seemed to be a good reason why we hadn't found just the right time for it. I suppose that ought to have warned me. I mean, it should have told me that she wasn't really serious about the project. Only I just preferred not to think about that. Next question?"

"My next question is just why you decided yesterday evening to leave last night." This time Roland did not pretend that the question was unimportant.

"Because I put it to her that I wasn't going to go on waiting," Jonathan said. "I told her I'd had enough of it."

"And this was in The Running Man?"

"Yes, it was."

"And isn't it a fact that it was she who telephoned you from there, asking you to join her? It was she who arranged that meeting, not you."

Jonathan looked puzzled. "Yes, it was."

"And what was her object?"

"I suppose to tell me she'd decided against leaving her husband. But I persuaded her—I thought I'd persuaded her—to come away with me after all. We arranged to meet at Heathrow sometime during the night or in the early morning, and get tickets on whatever plane we could. We didn't fix a definite time for meeting because she didn't know when she'd be able to slip out of the house. And I realise now that she gave in and agreed with everything I suggested much too easily. She never meant to go, she just saw that the easiest way to put me off was to agree to all I wanted."

"Yet she did leave her husband," Roland said.

"Yes."

"Do you know why?"

Jonathan did not reply at once, and when he did it was with a sound of reluctance.

"I'm only guessing, but I've a feeling it's connected with a belief she had that he was responsible for his father's death. Not that she exactly believed that, but she was haunted by an idea that it might be the truth. And she was determined not to give any evidence against him. Whether she actually had any evidence . . ." He paused and shrugged his shoulders. "I'm inclined to doubt it, but I really don't know."

"Didn't she telephone you in your office in the late afternoon of December the twenty-third, and didn't you leave the office immediately after her call instead of staying on for the Christmas party that was being held there that evening?"

Colin interrupted, "Inspector, I don't know where this is leading, but I'm beginning to feel that my son shouldn't answer any more of your questions without our solicitor being present."

"It's all right," Jonathan said, "I don't mind answering. Yes, it's quite true Gwen phoned me and said she wanted to talk to me, and we arranged to meet in The Running Man about six o'clock. But before we did, while I was on my way home, the bomb went off and of course we didn't have any meeting then."

"Did she say anything then about why she wanted to see you?"

"No, but of course it was to tell me the things she told me yesterday evening."

"Could it be that she was making sure that you would come along the lane at the usual time, instead of staying on for your office party for she didn't know how long?"

Jonathan drew in a shaky breath, staring at Roland incredulously.

"You're suggesting she planted the bomb in the lane to try to kill me!"

"No, only that she made that telephone call," Roland replied. "And she might have made it under some compulsion."

"What kind of compulsion were you thinking of, Inspector?" Andrew asked. "A gun in her back, for instance?"

"I've known stranger things than that happen," Roland said, and Sergeant Porter nodded his head vigorously as if to show that he too had had his experiences. "However, while agreeing that it doesn't sound too probable and forgetting it for the moment, it may interest you to know that we're holding Thomas Waterman and that he'll probably be charged with the murder of Sir Lucas Dearden. He's admitted now that he spoke on the telephone to Mr. Haslam in the afternoon of the twenty-third, asking him how he could get in touch with Sir Lucas, and that Mr. Haslam told him Sir Lucas was on his way home. That isn't exactly a confession, of course, and once he'd admitted it he announced he wasn't going to answer any more questions, but my guess is he'll end up by pleading guilty."

"Did Mr. Haslam come to see you and tell you about that telephone call?" Jonathan asked.

"Yes, and it was when he did that that Waterman admitted it was true," Roland said. "Well, I think that's all for now. I'm sorry to have troubled you." He looked at Andrew. "You're staying here for the present, are you, Professor?"

Suddenly Andrew wondered how much longer he would in fact be staying. The arrangement that he had originally made with the Cahills was that he should stay until December the twenty-eighth. The pressure of the holiday would have been over by then, and when he returned home shops would have opened and he would have been able to stock in supplies against the New Year siege. But now it was possible that he would be required to stay, though how he could be useful he did not know. However, he was one of the people who had heard the bomb explode and had been on the scene immediately after it. He might still be questioned, even though he had nothing to say, and at any rate to leave might draw unwelcome attention to himself. When the two detectives had gone, he thought, he would discuss the matter with Colin and Dorothea.

His answer to Roland's question was a vague nod, and Roland and the sergeant left a few minutes later.

Dorothea turned swiftly on Jonathan and said, "You never told us anything about that telephone call from Gwen to your office."

He gave a deep sigh and said, "No."

"Why didn't you?"

"Why should I?"

"No—no, of course there was no reason why you should."

She was looking more than usually distraught. "I'm in a muddle, that's all. The call was before all these awful things started happening, wasn't it? And Gwen couldn't have been expecting anything—"

"Mum!" Jonathan broke in. "What are you trying to say? Of course Gwen wasn't expecting anything."

At that moment the telephone shrilled.

Colin picked it up and said in an irritated tone, "Cahill speaking." Then he listened for a moment and said, "Hold on, he's just here." He turned to Andrew. "For you."

Andrew could not think who could be ringing him up at that number, but he went to Colin's side and took the telephone from him.

A woman's voice said quietly, "This is Lyn Goddard. I'd like to talk to you. Could you meet me in about a quarter of an hour in the bar of The Running Man?"

"I could," Andrew said, "but I'd feel happier about it if you gave me some idea what you want to talk about."

"I'd sooner not," she said. "I imagine you aren't alone in that room you're in, are you?"

"No."

"You couldn't talk freely at your end."

"Perhaps not."

"So let's say it had better keep till we meet. If a quarter of an hour isn't convenient, it could be later."

"A quarter of an hour will do."

"Thank you." She rang off.

Andrew put the telephone down and said, "That was Lyn Goddard. She wants me to go off immediately and meet her in The Running Man. She wouldn't say why, except that she wants to talk to me. Do any of you mind my going?"

"Of course not," Colin said. "It's your business."

"I'm not sure about that," Jonathan objected uneasily. "If there's something she knows, oughtn't she to tell it to us all? Perhaps the best thing would be if I went along with you."

"I don't think she wants that," Andrew said.

"If she did, she'd have said so, wouldn't she?" Colin said. "No, go along, Andrew. You'll know if she's got something to tell you that you think we ought to know."

Thankful for Colin's calm and good sense, Andrew put on his overcoat, took the torch and set off down the dark lane towards the village.

He could not resist lingering at the gate for a moment, sending the beam of the torch this way and that over the charred hedgerows near to where the burning car had stood. It would not take the hedges long, he thought, to regain their normal growth, and if any fragment of the car had been blasted into them or along the ground, these would all have been carefully collected and removed by the police. He doubted if such things would yield any clues. The solution of what had happened would probably be found in what a small group of people had to say about one another.

Had Lyn Goddard anything to say of any significance, he wondered, and why had she chosen him to talk to? One answer to that last question might simply be that both he and she were outsiders, not a part of the little world of Upper Cullonden. Or she might have the idea, as some people had, that he was clever and perceptive and able to give good advice. He shrank at the thought, but set off walking briskly towards the village.

He found her waiting for him in the lounge bar of The Running Man. There were only three or four other people in it. It was in the old part of the building and had a low, dark, beamed ceiling, small windows over which crimson curtains were drawn, a few low round tables with chairs around them and a narrow bar behind which stood a bald-headed man of immense portliness. This, Andrew supposed, was Joe Hobson of whom Colin had spoken, the man who had told him that Thomas Waterman was staying at the inn.

Lyn Goddard was sitting at one of the little tables. She had a glass before her which contained either gin and orange juice or plain orange juice. She raised a hand in a small gesture of greeting as Andrew went to the bar and ordered a whisky and soda. She was wearing a tweed coat over the same grey dress she had worn on all the occasions he had seen her. She wore no make-up on her pale, calm face.

Andrew brought his whisky to her table and sat down facing her.

"Well, here I am," he said.

"Yes," she acknowledged. "It was good of you to come. Did the Cahills mind my asking you to come?"

"If they did, they didn't say so."

"So you think they did."

"I think they mind everything that's happened since that bomb blast. A little more mystery is neither here nor there. But of course you've your reason for wanting to see me. I hope it's something I'm going to be able to tell them about, because we're very old friends and keeping something rather obviously to myself isn't going to be easy. So I rather hope you aren't going to tell me anything in confidence."

"I see." She fingered her glass and gazed, not at him, but slightly to one side of him with a wide, unfocussed stare. "I'll have to leave it to you how much you tell them. I don't want to insist on anything. But isn't it a fact that they believe Gwen and Jonathan were going away together?"

"I think so, yes."

"Only it isn't true, you see."

She was still avoiding looking at him, and for once there was an expression of uncertainty on the face that was usually so quietly confident.

"Is that something you know for sure, or is it just something you've guessed?" he asked.

"I know it for sure—well, almost for sure," she answered. "In the end it's pretty well impossible to know what other people are going to do, isn't it?"

"Pretty nearly, if not quite always," he agreed. "You don't think she ever intended to meet Jonathan at Heathrow?"

"I'm certain she didn't."

"Why?"

"Because she isn't in the least in love with him. She's deeply, you might say almost desperately, in love with Nicholas. It's Nicholas who isn't in love with Gwen. He's in love with me."

She met his eyes at last, and he had no doubt of her sincerity.

"And she knows this, does she?" he asked.

"Oh yes," she said. "That was why she wanted Nicholas to agree to live abroad. It was to get him away from me."

"Since when has she known it?"

"For about the last year."

"Yet she invited you here for Christmas."

"Yes, but it was Nicholas who insisted on that. He wanted things to be cleared up amongst the three of us. And Sir Lucas wasn't going to be here. We'd never have managed to get anywhere if he'd been there to interfere. Gwen would have confided in him and he'd have bullied Nicholas in the way he usually did and Nicholas would have given in. He's a —a very yielding sort of person."

She might as easily have said a weak one, but it seemed she loved him in spite of it. Perhaps she felt she had enough strength for the two of them.

"You and he—forgive the question—have been lovers, have you, and Gwen accepted this rather than give Nicholas up?" Andrew said.

"As a matter of fact, no, we haven't been lovers," she answered. "Nicholas wouldn't leave her as long as she held on to him so frantically. He said he couldn't hurt her so much. And I wasn't ready for one of those shared relationships."

He wondered whether or not to believe her. He drank some whisky, then after a moment asked, "Why are you telling me all this?"

"Because I'm really worried about her," she said. "What's really happened to her? And because I don't want you to think that Nicholas had any motive for harming Jonathan. If she'd left him it would have been the best possible thing for Nicholas. If the bomb in the lane was intended for Jonathan, it wasn't Nicholas who put it there."

"Have you any idea then who it could have been?"

"No, but I don't know a great deal about Jonathan. He may have all sorts of enemies."

"Suppose it wasn't Jonathan who was the target. Suppose the bomb was always meant for Dearden."

"And you still think it could have been Nicholas . . ." She gave a little gasp. "That's what Gwen thought at first. She thought he wanted money so that he could give up his writing and go away with me, but provide for her at the same time. That's why she was frightened of him and screamed when he went near her. So many things pointing to him! And you probably think, no smoke without fire."

"I believe there are all sorts of ways of producing smoke without fire nowadays, just as you can have fire without smoke," Andrew said. "At the moment I've no suspicions of Nicholas, though it's true that now he's a rich man and he can stop writing spy stories if the fact is that he isn't much interested in them. But there's something you seem to have forgotten. It was your statement that there was no telephone call to the Deardens' house on the day of the bomb, and I, for one, have felt inclined to believe you. But you've just made some more statements which make it very easy for one to assume that if there'd been a call to Nicholas during the day, telling him that his father was on the way home, you'd have done your very best to cover up the fact."

She considered what he had said, then shook her head. "I didn't. There was no call."

"Well, what do you want me to do now?" he asked. "Not, presumably, tell what you've been telling me to the police. Yet somehow you want me to use it to clear Nicholas. Have you any suggestions about that, because if there's any way I can help, I'll do what I can."

"You haven't any ideas of your own about it?"

"I'm sorry, no."

Suddenly she looked vulnerable and unsure of herself, almost as if she might start to cry.

"I thought you'd have some idea, now that you know so much," she said shakily. "I thought you've so much understanding, you'd be sure to be able to help us. I thought if I confided in you you'd be sure to be able to tell me what I ought to do."

Andrew felt the shrinking sensation that usually assailed him if anyone accused him of being wise.

Reluctantly, wishing that he need not answer at all, he said what seemed to him to commit him least.

"All that I can suggest is that you should wait and see. After all, things haven't got very far yet, have they? We don't know what the police may have uncovered by now, for one thing. I think if I were you I'd be inclined not to tell what you've told me to anyone else. A time may come when you'll have to talk about it, but I don't think that time is yet."

"But if you think it could be Nicholas . . ." She broke off as the door into the bar opened and Henry Haslam came in.

He came to their table. His face was sternly grave. Standing over them, looking massively stout but at the same time formidable, he said, "I was told I'd find you here. They've found Gwen. Her body was in one of those tool-sheds on the allotments. It had been there for some hours. She'd been strangled."

EIGHT

HE DROPPED INTO A CHAIR at the table and Andrew immediately said, "Whisky? Brandy?"

"Whisky, please," Haslam said.

Andrew went to the bar. When he returned with the drink Lyn was sitting rigidly still, her eyes on Haslam's face with a fascinated stare of incredulity.

Abruptly she said, "No!"

"Oh yes, they found her only a little while after the police were notified that she was missing," Haslam said. "One of the allotment holders went up to do a job of work on his patch, opened his tool-shed and there she was. He bolted back to the village and phoned the police only a short time after Nicholas had been in touch with them. They've been at the house for some time now, asking questions. Awkward thing, you see, they'd taken Waterman in for questioning about Lucas's death and had him all set as the murderer. He'd got motive, opportunity, everything. But he can't have had anything to do with Gwen's death because he was at the police station all night. Perfect alibi. No, even though he knew Lucas was coming home because of what I told him on the phone, he'd nothing to do with Gwen's murder. Not possibly. Very awkward. Damndest thing."

"Do they know about when she was killed?" Andrew asked, aware that he was taking this news unnaturally calmly, which was dangerous. He would have to pay for it later.

"Oh, they're very vague about it as usual," Haslam said. "Around one or two in the morning, they seem to think, give or take an hour or two. And it looks as if the only person with any motive to kill her is Nicholas. Everything seems to pile up against poor old Nicholas. I wouldn't like to be in his shoes."

Andrew became aware that Lyn was trembling, but her voice was steady as she said, "Are you suggesting he killed her because he discovered she was about to leave him with Jonathan?"

"What else?" Haslam said.

"I've just explained to Professor Basnett what else," she said. "Nothing could have pleased Nicholas more than if Gwen had decided to leave him for anyone under the sun. Nicholas wanted Gwen to divorce him so that he and I could get married. And if you're going to suggest he might have killed her because she wouldn't agree to a divorce, I can only say you don't live in the modern world. If she'd refused to divorce him he'd have ended up by leaving her, and he and I could have settled down together comfortably enough without benefit of clergy or registrar."

Haslam's mouth dropped open a little as he gazed at her.

"Nicholas and you . . . !" he stammered.

"Yes, Nicholas and me," she said.

Andrew was watching her uneasily, wishing that her impenetrability, which had been briefly shattered a little while ago, had not returned in so chilling a fashion.

"Didn't you say to me that Nicholas wouldn't leave Gwen

because he couldn't face hurting her so much?" he asked. "You did say something like that."

"Yes, and it's quite true," she said. "But I don't think I ever implied that murdering her would be a way of avoiding hurting her."

"Then—then it's you that has the motive!" Haslam exclaimed, still stuttering. "If Nicholas wouldn't leave Gwen unless she agreed to it, and she wouldn't, and you—you were here last night—if he wouldn't go away with you . . . I beg your pardon, I'm getting carried away. Of course I don't mean a word of it."

"But you do," she said gently. "I'm the perfect suspect for Gwen's murder. That's obvious. Don't you think so, Andrew?" She turned a singularly sweet smile on him.

Hurriedly he drank some of his whisky.

"Well, perhaps, Lyn," he said. "I suppose you might have become so exasperated with Gwen for keeping hold of Nicholas that you'd . . . But no, one doesn't kill a person out of exasperation. There has to be a stronger motive than that."

"Oh, I've often thought of murdering her," she said. "I'll admit it."

"Let me advise you not to say that to the police," Haslam said gravely. "Here, among friends, one can take it as it's meant, but for your own sake, take my advice, be careful."

Andrew marvelled at the speed with which the three of them, who had met only very recently and very briefly, were supposed to have become friends who could confide in one another.

"But I meant it just as I said," Lyn said in the same gentle tone as before. It made Andrew more afraid of her than it had occurred to him to be till then. "I've lain awake and dreamt about it. I've picked up a heavy hammer and swung it through the air and wondered if I could ever bring myself to crash it down on her skull. I've felt the edge of a carving knife and wondered if it was sharp enough to cut a throat or be plunged into a heart."

"And perhaps you picked up some nylon washing-line and thought how easy it would be to tighten it round a throat," Andrew suggested, feeling that for the moment the easiest thing would be to fall in with her mood. "You did say Gwen was strangled, didn't you, Haslam? What with?"

"A strong pair of hands, apparently," Haslam said. He looked from Andrew to Lyn with a frown, as if he had just caught them making some incomprehensible jokes. "Lyn has quite small hands, I observe. I don't think they could have done this thing."

Lyn held up her hands in front of her, spreading out the fingers. They were long and slender and did not look very strong.

"My hands have let me down," she said. "I shall never get into the history books. I mean those books that so often get written about brides in the bath, and Crippen, and Palmer and all those people. I'm glad we've sorted that out. For a little while I was worried."

For the first time Andrew became aware of the intensity of her concern, even though it was not for herself, but for Nicholas.

"You were never the best of suspects," he said, "unless you've taken some private tuition in the making of bombs. I suppose you don't claim to have done that."

"No, but I don't see why you should assume that the two crimes were committed by the same person," she said. "I think it's obvious Waterman obtained and planted the bomb. Then someone else murdered Gwen. Perhaps an accomplice of Waterman's, because Gwen had somehow found out too much. A man like Waterman may only have been someone else's tool, planting the bomb to kill Lucas or Jonathan and getting well paid for it."

"But if you're right, don't you think Waterman will talk as soon as the police start to put pressure on him?" Andrew said. "And that would make the murder of Gwen a bit super-

fluous. In fact, only adding more danger to an already very
dangerous situation."

"So you still believe it was Nicholas!" Her voice suddenly
cracked, turning high and shrill, completely changing its
usual pleasant, low-pitched quality. "You've made up your
minds! You won't listen! Well, I'll tell them who the murderer really is, because I know! I've kept quiet because it
seemed only the decent thing to do, but if they're going to try
and put this thing on Nicholas . . ." She sprang up from her
chair. Her face had flamed and her eyes were burning with
fury that seemed to be directed at Haslam. "I'm going to the
police now and I'm going to tell them everything I know!"

Tripping over the leg of one of the chairs at the table and
almost falling in her haste to be gone, she darted out of the
bar.

The door slammed shut behind her. One or two people in
the bar looked up at her violent departure with a show of
slight curiosity, but Andrew did not think that either he or
she had been recognized as people connected with the Cahills
or the Deardens; there would have been far more interest
taken in them.

Haslam got to his feet. "Another drink!" he proclaimed.
"You too?"

He walked away to the bar without waiting for Andrew's
answer.

Returning with whisky for them both and sitting down
again, he said, "What did she mean by that? Do you think she
really knows anything about how these awful things happened?"

"I've got my doubts," Andrew said, "but she may think she
does."

"I always liked Gwen, you know," Haslam said. "I felt
sorry for her." He paused. "Do you think Lyn was telling the
truth about her and Nicholas?"

"Well, I wondered about that, but I think it was true. She
was doing her best to clear Nicholas of any suspicion that he

might have wanted to get rid of Jonathan out of jealousy over an affair he was supposed to be having with Gwen. According to Lyn there was no affair, except for a rather frustrated sort of one between herself and Nicholas."

Haslam shook his head dubiously.

"I don't understand these young people nowadays," he said. "They seem to think marriage is all fun and games. No sense of responsibility. I don't like it. I may be old-fashioned, but I don't like it. Marriage should be a very serious thing."

"But why were you sorry for Gwen?" Andrew asked.

"Because old Lucas bullied and exploited her abominably. He'd no regard for her. I'm not sure who her parents were, and she'd no money of her own and not much in the way of brains or education, and Lucas always made it clear he thought Nicholas had married beneath him."

"That's rather the impression I got from reading Dearden's memoirs," Andrew said. "She's barely mentioned in them."

"You've read the memoirs, have you?" There was a sudden flash of interest on Haslam's ruddy face.

"Yes," Andrew said.

"What did you make of them?"

"One of the dullest things I've ever had to read."

"Nothing to tell you why anyone should want to blow him up with a bomb?"

"Not a thing."

"I daresay I shouldn't ask this, but is there anything particular about me in them?"

Andrew could see that the man hoped there was. If the book ever got into print and if it came into his hands, the first thing that he would do with it would be to look at the index to see if his name was mentioned there.

"A few remarks, all quite complimentary," Andrew said. "But of course it may never be published. A curious thing, though. He'd torn out one page after giving it to a woman here to be typed, and according to her that page referred mainly to you and your wife. Her idea about it was that he'd felt it was too personal."

Haslam frowned. "Critical of us, d'you mean? But you said it was fairly complimentary."

"Yes, it's probably of no importance whatever." As he said it Andrew seemed to hear Inspector Roland affirming that the questions that he was asking were of no importance. He stood up. "Hadn't we better be getting back? The police may be wanting to talk to us."

"I believe they may be." Haslam finished his drink and stood up too. "As a matter of fact, I slipped out before they realised what I was going to do. It was Nicholas who dropped a word in my ear. Now that we know about him and Lyn, I suppose it was Lyn he wanted."

"So he knew she was coming here to talk to me. I wonder if he put her up to it."

They made for the door. The night outside was very dark. There was neither moonlight nor starlight, only heavy clouds that moved sluggishly across the sky, blackening it. There was a feeling of moisture in the air which, though not quite rain, spread a little prickling chill on Andrew's skin.

As he switched on the torch that he had brought with him, he wondered if he was walking back to Stillmore Lane with a double murderer. Granted that Henry Haslam could not have blown up Lucas Dearden himself. He had been in London and able to answer the telephone when Nicholas had rung him up to tell him of the horror in the lane. But according to Haslam's own admission, he had been in touch with Waterman and had told him that Dearden was on his way home. The question was, had Haslam simply given Waterman that information, or had he given him instructions too? And had Gwen, during her visit to Erica in the London hospital, learnt more about this than was safe for her, and if she had, had she threatened Haslam with exposure? It might explain why he had remained in Upper Cullonden the night before, relying on borrowed pyjamas, razor and toothbrush.

But how could he have known that she would not be going to bed at the normal time and that she would be available, as you might put it, for strangulation in the middle of the night?

Suppose, then, that she had not threatened him, but had confided in him, waiting until after Nicholas had gone upstairs to his drugged sleep to tell Haslam her troubles? But he had not trusted her to keep her knowledge to herself; and he was big and strong and could easily have crushed her slender neck and carried her small body up to a tool-shed on the allotments. It all fitted rather neatly.

But do you ask for help and advice from someone who, you have recently learnt, has just murdered your father-in-law?

Perhaps if you hated that father-in-law enough yourself. To whom would you sooner turn with your difficulties than his murderer?

There was still the question of whether or not Henry Haslam had had any motive for killing Lucas Dearden. Andrew could not think of one, knowing really as little as he did about the man. He was said to have money, to have a beautiful wife and to have been on the best of terms with Dearden. A fortunate man, one would say, unlikely to be driven to dangerous violence. All the same, he had had the opportunity to commit two murders.

"Bloody unseasonable weather," Haslam remarked as he and Andrew turned into Stillmore Lane. "We'll pay for it later, mark my words."

"At least it's shortened the winter a little," Andrew said, "even if the worst is still to come."

"Didn't the great freeze-up of '47 start only around February?" Haslam said. "Of course I was only a kid then, and I remember enjoying it immensely, tobogganing and skating and all that. It didn't worry me that my parents were being driven nearly out of their minds by frozen pipes. Then when the thaw came we had a flood. The main pipe was burst in the roof and water came pouring down the walls and brought great chunks of the ceilings crashing down. As far as I can remember, I took it all as a great adventure. God, how I wish we hadn't got to face the police now, but poor Gwen, it's all we can do for her. Hell, it's starting to rain."

The cold moisture that Andrew had felt on his face was certainly changing to heavier drops. He and Haslam hastened their steps. By the time they reached the Cahills' house a thin but steady rain was falling. Shivering a little, Andrew had turned up his collar against it, but felt the drops wetting his hair and sliding down his neck. His own words had been echoing in his mind as he walked along. "The worst is still to come . . ." Asking himself if anything could be worse than what had already come, his answer was that of course it could. In evil, it often appears, there are no limits. Muttering good-bye to Haslam as he turned in at the Cahills' gate while Haslam went on to the Deardens', he felt a deep dissatisfaction with himself because he understood so little about what had happened.

He found Dorothea, Colin and Jonathan in the sitting-room with drinks in their hands. Colin immediately offered one to Andrew, which in spite of what he had had in The Running Man he was glad to accept. But first he wanted to go upstairs to rub his hair with a towel and change out of his muddy shoes into slippers. When presently he returned to the sitting-room all three Cahills stared at him in an almost challenging way, as if they were sure that there was something he could tell them.

When he said nothing, Colin said, "You've heard about Gwen, of course."

"Yes," Andrew said.

"From Lyn?" Colin asked. "Did she know about it?"

"No," Andrew answered. "We heard about it from Haslam, who came along to the pub to collect us. Have the police been here?"

"No, but we've been over at the Deardens'. Nicholas rang up at once to tell us what had happened and we went over

there to see if there was anything we could do, but Roland
sent us away. He said he'd be coming here later."

"Are you sure Lyn didn't know about it?" Jonathan asked.
There was a tremor in his voice and his face was unusually
drawn. "She and Henry were in the house when Gwen
slipped out. They must have been. I'm not accusing anyone
of anything except perhaps of knowing more than they're
letting on, but doesn't that seem likely?"

"Possible, anyway," Andrew said.

"If Nicholas didn't really swallow the sleeping pills Gwen
gave him, or if they had no effect on him," Jonathan went on
rapidly, "if he went out after her and they know he did,
mightn't Lyn try to cover up for him?"

"According to her, there was nothing to cover up," Andrew said. "She says Nicholas is in love with her and nothing
would have pleased him better than if Gwen had decided to
go away with you."

A dull flush covered Jonathan's face. "That isn't true! God,
if it had been, how easy everything would have been! For one
thing, I don't suppose old Lucas would have got murdered in
mistake for me."

"Only Gwen didn't go away with you," Andrew said.

"And now we know why, don't we?"

"What about her handbag?" Andrew asked.

Jonathan looked puzzled and Colin said, "What's her handbag got to do with it?"

A sense of extraordinary weariness suddenly assailed Andrew. He had noticed this happening to him increasingly
lately, a feeling of exhaustion overcoming him almost as intensely as a blow. He leant back in his chair, sipped his drink
and gave a deep sigh.

"Just a thought," he said. "We've been told she didn't take a
suitcase with her when she disappeared, but did take her
handbag. Well, of course if she was strangled in the house
and carried out to the allotments, it's obvious why she hadn't
a suitcase with her, but it would be interesting to know why

she had her handbag. Did she keep tight hold of it while she was being strangled, or is our murderer a more than usually thoughtful character, doing his best to attend to details? Incidentally, was there any money in it?"

"Seven hundred and fifty pounds and some loose cash," Colin answered.

"Quite a sum to be wandering around with in the dark. Where was it found?"

"In the shed beside her."

"So she wasn't attacked and robbed as she went to the garage for her car, or anything like that."

"Obviously not," Jonathan said impatiently. "And I tell you this story about Nicholas and Lyn is sheer fantasy."

"Supper!" Dorothea suddenly called.

She hustled them out to the kitchen where a cold meal had been laid on the table. They were still eating some of the cold beef left over from the Christmas dinner, but the mince pies were finished and the beef was followed by the usual bread and cheese. She apologized for it a little incoherently, saying that she had meant to make a steak and kidney pie for that evening, but somehow had not been able to bring herself to concentrate on it.

"But I'll make it tomorrow, I really will," she said. "I'm ashamed at the way I've been feeding you, Andrew. You'll never come again."

Andrew wondered if he would in fact ever be able to brace himself for another visit to Upper Cullonden, but that was not on account of the diet that he had received there. Then as he looked at Colin's plump, oval face with its pink, rounded cheeks and big, blue, thoughtful and observant eyes, and then at Dorothea's fragile-looking smallness, her fine-boned features and shy, gentle eyes, he knew that if they wanted him to come again, he would come.

But perhaps his presence would remind them of what they would need to forget quite as badly as he would, and there would be no invitation. Next Christmas might find them in the West Indies or California or somewhere far away. But if so, would Jonathan be with them? What was going to become of him now? It was probable, Andrew thought, that the construction firm in Rockford would not have him on their books much longer. He was in the state of mind when a job abroad might have a certain appeal. Something well-paid, even if possibly dangerous, in, say, the Middle East. Anyway, something a long, long way from Upper Cullonden and the parents to whom he had hitherto been so happy to cling.

Supper was finished and the washing-up done by the time Detective Inspector Roland and Sergeant Porter arrived. Both men looked tired, and they did not refuse the whisky that Colin offered them. They sank into comfortable chairs with looks of relief, as if they both felt that they had been on their feet for far too long and could do with a rest.

Roland looked at Andrew and observed, "Told you there was a depression coming, didn't I? They got it right for once. And now the forecast is frost. So if this rain goes on we'll all be sliding around tomorrow on the ice. That's something I've never liked driving on. Don't trust myself not to get into a skid. Luckily Bob here's an excellent driver."

The sergeant looked even more pleased than he usually did. Though tired, he gave the impression of having had a happy day.

Roland, however, once he had made the obligatory remarks about the weather, looked irritable.

"Mr. Cahill," he said, addressing not Colin, but Jonathan, "I'd be grateful if you'd bring your mind to bear on the question of any enemies who might be after your blood. Could you mention one or two?"

Before Jonathan could answer, Andrew said, "If you're thinking of Mr. Dearden, I don't believe he had any motive for killing Jonathan Cahill."

"Ah, you've been listening to Miss Goddard," Roland said. "She's been telling us Mr. Dearden had nothing against him. There was nothing between him and Mrs. Dearden, so she says, and if there had been, Mr. Dearden wouldn't have cared. All right, suppose that's true; what I was really asking young Mr. Cahill is if he's got any suspicions of anybody else?"

"No," Jonathan said.

"No one at all?"

"No." Jonathan sounded surly.

"What were your relations with Mr. Haslam?" Roland asked.

"Henry!" Jonathan made a curious noise in his throat which might have been a smothered laugh. "Don't tell me you're thinking Henry could be a murderer. He's virtue itself."

"We've got to think of everyone," Roland said, "and he's the one person we know of who had the opportunity to commit both murders. He'd Waterman to do the one job for him, and he was here last night himself and could have done the other."

"But if he was using Waterman," Andrew said, "wouldn't it suggest his target was Sir Lucas, not Jonathan Cahill?"

"That's right, it would," Roland said as if this fact had been too obvious for him to mention it. "All the same, we're short of a motive there. Naturally Haslam's financial standing will be investigated, but unless he's got himself into trouble that none of you know of and needed money, it's difficult to see what he had to gain by Sir Lucas's death. From the look of things, they were on good terms with one another. Sir Lucas was going to spend Christmas with Mr. and Mrs. Haslam and would have done it if she hadn't had her accident. That looks as if they got on all right. But what about you, Mr. Cahill?" He surveyed Jonathan, his thick eyelids drooping so that his wide-spaced eyes looked as if he wanted to conceal the glitter in them. "I'd like to know more about your relations with Mr. Haslam. But going back to Mr. Dearden, we know you waited at Heathrow, presumably for Mrs. Dearden. That's been checked. But she didn't join you, although that's what you say you'd arranged, for the simple reason, we know now, that she'd been murdered. It wasn't that she was stringing you along, never intending to join you, as has been suggested to me. And there isn't much mystery about why she didn't pack a suitcase, though that's been thought strange. She was probably killed before she got around to doing it. So it looks as if it must have been someone in the house who did it, and we're back to Mr. Dearden, aren't we? Wouldn't you call him an enemy of yours, Mr. Cahill?"

"I don't think I'm going to answer that," Jonathan said.

Colin nodded his head in approval.

"In case you're interested, we've taken him in for questioning," Roland told them. "We may call on you for a statement about your relations with Mrs. Dearden."

"What about her handbag?" Andrew asked.

He was conscious that he had asked the question not long before and must seem to have handbags on the brain, as a little while ago he had had passports. But he had not received any answer that had satisfied him.

"Ah, the handbag," Roland said. "Interesting you should have thought of that. Curious point. She's going to start packing, or perhaps she's actually started, when she's taken hold of from behind—we know it was from behind—and the life's squeezed out of her. And then, if she's started packing, her murderer carefully unpacks her case and hangs up her things as usual and carries her out to the allotments. And he takes her handbag with him and leaves it beside her in the shed, with a fair amount of money in it. It seems that money was mostly her husband's. She'd helped herself to all he had in his wallet, which he was in the habit of keeping pretty well stocked. But why did he take the handbag out with her? Ask me another! He must have known her body would be found pretty soon, so the fact that her handbag was missing from the house wouldn't have signified anything much. My own guess is it was one of those pointless little bits of elaboration that sometimes give criminals away. He was used to seeing her with a handbag. It almost seemed a part of her. So when he carried her out he just took her handbag along as a matter of course. Naturally it's been tested for fingerprints, and that's interesting. There are her husband's prints on it as well as Mrs. Dearden's."

Dorothea produced one of her sudden explosions into speech. "That doesn't mean anything! If you tested my handbag for fingerprints, you'd find mine and my husband's and my son's on it. Everyone in the house just helps themselves from it when they feel like it."

Roland smiled. "I believe it's the same in my own home. My wife has more time to go to the bank and cash a cheque than I have, and the money stays in her handbag till I want some."

"So you're married, Inspector," Dorothea said, almost as if she did not believe it.

"Yes," he said.

"Have you any children?"

"Just the two."

"How old are they?"

"Hugh's seven, Eileen's five."

He looked a little bemused by her rapid-fire questions, but plainly did not want to be discourteous.

"Does Hugh want to go into the police when he grows up?"

"An airline pilot is his ambition at present," he said, "but Eileen wants to go into the police."

"And is your wife interested in your work?"

"I suppose so. She's got her own interests."

"And what are they?"

The turn that the interrogation had taken seemed suddenly to overcome Sergeant Porter with a desire to giggle. He controlled it, but a broad grin spread over his wide, bland face.

Roland stood up. "We must be going. I'm sorry to have kept you so long. Thank you for your help."

"But what does your wife do while you're working?" Dorothea insisted. "I mean, you haven't a nine to five job, have you? It must be very difficult for her, for instance, to arrange good meals for you."

"She manages," he said.

"Has she a job? Please forgive my questions. I'm always so interested in the way other people manage their lives. You know, years ago I took a degree in sociology. That's when I met my husband, when we were both students. But I never tried to get a job in it because I didn't think I'd ever manage to keep a job and look after my home as well. Has your wife a job?"

"She does part-time in a café," he answered, beginning to look a little desperate and edging towards the door. "Professor, I wouldn't worry about that handbag. It probably isn't important. Come along, Bob."

Roland's remark that the handbag was not important made Andrew immediately sure, not only that it was, but that Roland was sure of this too. As Colin saw the two detectives out of the house, Andrew turned to Dorothea.

"You did that very nicely," he said. "You'd had enough of them, had you?"

She looked surprised. "I don't know what you mean, Andrew. I'm always interested in other people's work and I've often wondered about policemen and what goes on in their private lives. They're so important to us, yet most of us know hardly anything about them."

"You might ask Hugh and Eileen to tea, then you'd find out a lot about their father," Andrew said.

"Now you're laughing at me," she said reproachfully, "but I'm serious. I'm always interested in the work people do. Take Nicholas, for instance. Those spy stories he writes. They're very clever and they're simply overflowing with sex and violence, yet I never felt there was much sex in his relationship with Gwen and he always seemed so gentle; so I said to myself that he only wrote about things that were a bit lacking in his make-up, things he somehow needed to handle in his imagination because they weren't there in reality. And look how wrong I seem to have been. I'm afraid I'm very often wrong about people, though I think about them so much."

"You can't be sure you've been wrong about Nicholas," Andrew said.

"But if they've taken him in for questioning!"

"That isn't the same as charging him. And charging him isn't the same as finding him guilty. He's innocent till he's proved guilty, remember."

"But they wouldn't make a mistake like that. Or would they?" She turned her head and looked at Jonathan. "What do you really believe, darling?"

Instead of answering, he suddenly strode from the room, slamming the door behind him. They could hear his steps as he sprang up the stairs, then the slam of his bedroom door.

Dorothea gave a little shudder. "It's terrible for him," she said. "He blames himself, I can tell. If it hadn't been for that affair with Gwen none of it would have happened."

"If there ever was an affair with Gwen," Andrew said.

"Oh, there was," she said. "Lyn's only trying to cover up for Nicholas. You don't mean to say you believe her, do you?"

"Don't you?"

"Not for a moment. I told you about Jonathan and Gwen the other day, didn't I? I've known about that for some time. And I don't believe there's ever been anything between Lyn and Nicholas. Perhaps on her side, but not on his."

"In The Running Man she said she knew who'd done the murder," Andrew said, "and I don't think she meant Nicholas. But she sounded rather convincing."

Dorothea shook her head. "She isn't a person I feel inclined to believe. That icy sort of self-control she has . . . I think she'd say whatever she thought was most useful."

"You don't like her?"

"Well, I prefer people who are more spontaneous, but I wouldn't go so far as to say I don't like her. I don't often really dislike people, because, as I told you, I'm so interested in them, and nearly always, if you try, you can find something that's worth while—" She broke off as the door opened and Colin and Lyn Goddard came into the room.

Dorothea stood up quickly and said, "Lyn!" It sounded as if there could be no one whom she would be more pleased to see.

Lyn was in an overcoat and was carrying a plastic shopping-bag.

"I'm afraid this is a fearful intrusion," she said, "and if you want me to go away, please say so. But Colin said I could stay."

"Of course she can," Colin said. "She'll have to put up with the little room in the attic, but we can easily make up the bed for her there."

"You're staying the night?" Dorothea asked. She did not seem at all put out by the prospect, in spite of what she had been saying. "Of course we can put you up."

Lyn held up the shopping-bag. "I only brought a few things, just for the night. It's because that awful house frightens me, now that I'm alone in it. I won't mind it in the morning. They've taken Nicholas away, as I expect you know, and Henry's gone back to London to see how Erica's getting on, and the whole place is empty. I'm not usually like this. I'm hardly ever afraid of being alone. Really I rather like it. But there's something about that house now . . ." She shivered.

"Of course, of course," Dorothea said. "Take your coat off and come and have a drink and I'll go up and make up the bed for you. I'm so glad you decided to come. If I'd thought of your being alone there I'd have come over to ask you to spend the night with us, and to stay on, if that would help.

But the police have only just left us and I haven't got around to thinking about anything very clearly."

Andrew believed that the warmth of her welcome was not hypocritical. Lyn might not be one of the people she liked best, but still she was someone in trouble—and with problems about which it might be very intriguing to speculate.

Lyn took off her coat and Colin took it from her. Then she came to the fire and sat down beside it while Colin once more started pouring out drinks. Dorothea shot out of the room and went running up the stairs, presumably to the attic to make up the bed there. Andrew wondered if it would be a courtesy on his part to offer Lyn the good spare bedroom on the first floor, which he had been occupying, but thought that changing rooms would only make more work for everyone than letting things remain as they were.

"We were talking about you just before you arrived," he said. "I told Dorothea what you said in the pub, that you knew who'd done the murders. And didn't you say you were going to tell the police what you knew? Did you do that?"

She gave a small, sardonic smile. "What do you think?"

"Then you didn't?"

"And I don't know who did the murders either," she said. "It was just hysteria. You and Henry seemed so sure of yourselves, I couldn't stand it."

"I'm sorry," Andrew said. "Actually I'm not sure of anything."

"But Henry's sure, isn't he? He's written Nicholas off."

"Perhaps he has."

"You know, I'm glad he's gone home," she said. "Even if I had to spend the night alone in that house, I'd prefer it to spending it there with Henry."

"But why?" Colin asked. "I always thought he was a good sort of chap."

"That's what everyone thinks, isn't it?" she said.

"Well, isn't it true?" he said. "You aren't frightened of good old Henry, are you?"

"Good old Henry, I believe, is a very violent sort of man," she said. "Does that surprise you?"

"What's given you that idea?" he asked.

Her smile reappeared. It was not at all a friendly smile. But she answered in a quiet voice, "Just hysteria again, I expect. Letting my intuitions run away with me. Except for reading me a lecture after the police left with Nicholas about everything being my fault and how he despised women like me who had no regard for the sanctity of marriage, he's never been anything but very pleasant to me. But actually I believe he's the sort of man who probably has day-dreams of rape. He's just a mass of frustration and aggression, dressed up as that image of being good old Henry—" She broke off. "No, don't listen to me. I don't mean it. He got on my nerves, that's all. He's the sort of man who thinks that having a good bank account will cover everything. If you've got that you don't need to have imagination, or sympathy, or under-standing. How Erica's put up with him all this time I can't even guess."

"Perhaps she likes money too," Andrew suggested.

"Well, I like it myself," she said. "I'd like to have a lot of it. Lots and lots. But I'd be sorry if it was ever thought that it was the only virtue I had."

"I wonder what you think your virtues are," Andrew said.

Her smile this time looked less ironic. "That was a jab! I really sound so self-satisfied, do I?"

He did not think that she was at all self-satisfied. Her trouble, he thought, was that she was deeply dissatisfied with herself. What she wanted to appear and what she was were very different, and she knew it. She suffered from her knowl-edge of herself.

She went to bed early after apologizing several times to Dorothea for the trouble she was causing, and thanking her and Colin for their kindness to her. Andrew went to bed soon after her. He felt extremely tired, so tired that it would not be surprising, he thought, if the feeling should never abate. It seemed to him something that he might be doomed to endure for the rest of his days, of which, after all, there might not be very many left.

In bed he turned on the lamp beside him and settled down once more to his Rex Stout. He expected to fall asleep over it almost at once, but instead he found himself uncomfortably wakeful. He went on reading for more than an hour, thankful to be alone in the quiet room with no one asking questions to which he felt that he ought to know the answer, even if they were not addressed to him. He had reached the point in the story when Rex Stout's arch-detective, Nero Wolfe, had begun to suck his lips in and out, showing that his mind was very actively at work, before it seemed reasonable to turn the light out and see if sleep would come.

It did not come. In the darkness Andrew felt more wide awake than ever, and found it difficult even to close his eyes. Though tonight he did not see flames flickering around him or hear the explosion of a bomb, he found it all too easy to imagine a scene in the house next door in which a strong pair of hands closed around the throat of helpless Gwen Dearden, and then strong arms carried her limp body out to the shed on the allotments.

Whose hands? Whose arms?

It seemed imperative to answer those questions if he wanted to sleep. He wanted sleep very badly. But to want it too much, he knew, was always a mistake, and since he had never found counting sheep a very satisfactory sedative, he let his mind stray over the events of the last few days, only to find himself presently muttering to himself:

> Heap on more wood!—the wind is chill,
> But let it whistle as it will,
> We'll keep our Christmas merry still . . .

There was something infuriating about that. Why, after the terrible experiences of this Christmas, should he be plagued by lines of such complete unimportance? However, he knew that they would go round and round in his head unless he escaped into sleep or drove himself to think of some others instead.

Sleep, after a little while, felt as if it might be coming. He was experiencing the pleasant sense of vacancy which comes just before unconsciousness takes over, when he was annoyed by the same nonsensical lines that had plagued him once before beginning to hammer at his brain.

I gotta phone,
You gotta phone,
All God's chillun got phones.
When I get to Heaven goin' to phone all my friends—

He suddenly sat bolt upright in his bed.
"All God's chillun got phones . . ."
With his eyes once more open wide, he stared before him into the darkness. Then, after a time, he lay back again. But not to sleep. Not this night.

NINE

AT HALF PAST SIX Andrew got up, and as no one seemed yet to be astir in the house, he went to the bathroom, had a shower and shaved, then returned to his bedroom. He got dressed, then sat down by the window to watch the slow dawn come.

The central heating had switched itself off for the night, but at seven o'clock it switched on again and the room became reasonably warm. The morning was fine but cold. There was a sparkling white frost on the grass and the bushes in the garden. The sky, turning by degrees to palest blue, was clear except for a few clouds that wandered across it, coloured a brilliant rose by the rising sun. It was a long time since Andrew had watched a dawn. Even in winter, when it came so late, he usually slept till there was daylight at the window.

He sat very still, thinking that dawn seen from the window of a London flat, with only roofs and curtained windows visible across an empty street, could have none of the peaceful beauty of this one; yet how satisfying it would feel to be in his own home now, even if he had had a sleepless night. He stood up and suddenly began to pack his suitcase. It took only a few minutes, and when it was done he put the suitcase by the door and returned to the chair by the window. It was full daylight now and the rosy clouds were only puffs of white, without the drama they had had at sunrise. But it was going to be a fine day. If the frost that Inspector Roland had told him was foretold had in fact come, confounding Roland's scepticism about the weathermen, it did not look too threatening.

At eight o'clock there was a tap at the door and Jonathan came in, carrying Andrew's breakfast tray. Seeing Andrew up and dressed, he raised his eyebrows.

"You're up early, aren't you?" he said. "Didn't you have a good night?" He put the tray down on a table beside Andrew's chair. "I didn't have much of one myself."

Andrew saw that the tray had been neatly arranged as usual, with coffee and toast and marmalade and a small cube of Cheddar cheese. But he said nothing, and Jonathan, giving him a troubled look, turned towards the door.

He was only a step away from it when Andrew said, "You killed them both, didn't you, Jonathan?"

Jonathan had his back to Andrew at that moment, and Andrew did not see his face, but he saw the young man's body suddenly go rigid. Then he turned slowly and came back towards Andrew. His face had the pallor of shock.

"What do you mean, both?" His voice was almost a whisper.

"Sir Lucas Dearden and Gwen Dearden."

"I don't understand," Jonathan said.

"Then I suppose I'll have to explain." Andrew picked up the cube of cheese and began to nibble it. "But sit down, Jonathan. This may take a little time."

He gestured towards a chair, but Jonathan stayed standing where he was.

"It'll take quite a bit of explaining," he said.

"I know that." Andrew poured out his coffee. "It all begins with Erica, doesn't it?"

"Erica? How does she come into it?"

"Because it's Erica you've been in love with for a long time, perhaps since you were a student in London and used to visit the Haslams' house from time to time. There was never anything between you and Gwen. Lyn Goddard was absolutely right about that."

As if there were a strange fascination in what Andrew was saying, something that drew him against his will, Jonathan moved nearer to him and sat down in the chair where he had refused to sit a moment before. His eyes were fixed unblinkingly on Andrew's face.

"That's completely untrue," he said. "We did our best to hide it, but somehow Nicholas found out about it. And I think my mother guessed. In fact, I think a rumour about it must have got around."

"And people said, 'There's no smoke without fire.' But in this case there was smoke without any fire at all. There was a rumour without the least foundation, one which I think you rather skilfully encouraged so that where there really was fire there wasn't any smoke. But Erica shouldn't have made that telephone call."

"What telephone call?"

"The one she made to your office before the office party and that brought you home to plant the bomb that killed Dearden. It wasn't Gwen who made that call, it was Erica. She told you that if you did it right away, before other people knew her father was coming home, it would be assumed that you were the real target and that would confuse everybody."

"You can't possibly prove a thing like that," Jonathan said. But there was a crack in his voice and the direct stare of his eyes was wavering, though he managed to go on almost calmly. "The last few days have been too much for you, Andrew. I'd get on with your breakfast if I were you and then go home."

"It's what I'm hoping to do," Andrew replied. It annoyed him that when he picked up the cup he had just filled with coffee his hand was shaking. He thought that if anything Jonathan was the more composed of the two of them, which was not as things should be. "It'll be easy enough to prove. Erica's in a private hospital, of course in a private room. And she's certainly got a phone by her bed. All private hospitals have phones by their patients' beds. And they keep a record of the calls their patients make so that they can charge them. If Erica made that call to Rockford, it'll be on their account."

Jonathan considered this thoughtfully, then gave a slight shrug of his shoulders.

"All right, suppose it's Erica I'm in love with, doesn't that tell you what really happened? You seem to have missed the point."

"I'll be glad if I have."

"I'll explain it. She did make that call, but it had nothing to do with bringing me home. It was only to chat about her accident and to wish me a merry Christmas and so on. She didn't want to ring me up while I was here at home because my parents would have heard me answering and might have guessed whom I was talking to. And it was rather important for us to be very careful about no one finding out about us because of Henry. He's a very dangerous man, Andrew. Don't you understand, he's the murderer? Only the first murder went wrong. He meant to get Waterman to plant the bomb where it would blow me up, but Lucas got there just ahead of me and so he got it. I don't know how Henry found out about Erica and me. I suppose someone saw us together sometime and talked about it, or perhaps she talked about it herself in the state of shock she was in after her accident. Perhaps she called out for me or something like that. Anyway, he's the man you want. I'm only a minor character."

"What about Gwen's murder?" Andrew asked.

"Quite simply, she threatened him," Jonathan said. "She'd been up to London and seen Erica, and I think Erica confided in her and Gwen told Henry she knew what he'd done and that she was going to the police next day. She was just giving him a chance, you see, for all our sakes, to get away. He'd lots of money. He could have taken off to one of those South American countries you were talking about that don't go in for extradition. But he didn't take the chance. He's infatuated with Erica, you know. He'd never leave her. So he strangled Gwen to stop her talking, pretty sure that Nicholas would get the blame."

"What a pity you didn't take off for South America when I advised you to go there," Andrew said. "I'm sorry, I don't believe you, Jonathan. Haslam is the one person who can't have had anything to do with planting the bomb in the lane. You understand me, don't you?"

Jonathan did not reply. He looked incredulous, or at least, Andrew thought, was doing his best to look incredulous.

"Don't you see, Haslam knew Dearden was on his way home," Andrew said. "He'd even have known approximately when he'd get here. He knows how long it takes to drive from London to Upper Cullonden. So he'd have known that Dearden would have been arriving at around the same time as you normally did. So whichever of you it was that he wanted to murder, he'd have known there was a good chance that he'd get the wrong one. No, I don't think you can involve Haslam in this. You've a better chance of making out a case against Nicholas, only he seems to have had no motive. Perhaps I ought to go back to the beginning and tell you how I see things."

Again Jonathan did not reply. But there had been a change in his expression. There was a certain boldness about him now, even of truculence. For a moment Andrew felt afraid of him, but thought that in his parents' house there was really no serious threat to him.

"I believe the murder of Lucas Dearden was as carefully

planned and cold-blooded a crime as I've ever heard of," he said. "I don't know which of you thought of it, you or Erica. Probably you worked it out between you. You were in love with each other and she could easily have left Henry, but it happened that Erica liked money. She'd got used to it, living with a wealthy father and then with an equally wealthy husband. A husband, incidentally, who wouldn't have forgiven her if she'd been unfaithful to him. And however promising you are in your work and however successful you may become eventually, it'll take time. She'd have had some years of relative poverty to endure before she could live in the way to which she was accustomed. But if her father died she'd inherit a considerable amount, and thinking of that missing page 96 in his memoirs, I think one can deduce she didn't love him."

"She hated him!" Jonathan suddenly exploded, then looked as if he wished that he had not spoken.

"I thought that might be the case," Andrew said. "The real love of her life was a married man, a good deal older than herself, who she thought would leave his wife and marry her. But he decided to stick to his wife and the two of them left for New Zealand. I've wondered, ever since I heard about that, if Dearden had anything to do with it. I don't suggest he actually bribed the man to give Erica up, I don't know anything about that. But I don't think he was the sort of man Dearden wanted as a son-in-law, and I think the missing page may have given away the fact that he had more to do with the break-up of the relationship than he later thought was advisable. Then there was another man, a not very successful actor, who was killed in a car crash. That must have been a relief to Dearden. He wouldn't have fitted too well into the family either. And almost at once she married Haslam, just the kind of man Dearden would have chosen for her. Perhaps he did choose him. And she accepted him because it was a way of getting away from home, but that didn't mean he was going to be the only love of her life. I've never met her, so of course I'm only guessing, but it seems to me she's probably irresponsible, not too faithful to anybody, and that may include you. It strikes me that she may have thought of you as a convenience, with your access in your work to explosives and your being able to live next door to her father without it seeming unnatural, and so having the chance to kill him when the suitable opportunity occurred. Do you want me to go on, Jonathan?"

"Yes, go on," Jonathan muttered. "You can't say anything much worse than you've said already."

"Well, the suitable opportunity happened to come when she had her accident," Andrew said. "Her father was coming to stay over Christmas with her and Haslam, but when she was taken into hospital he decided to come home. Haslam knew this and he told her. And as soon as she could she telephoned you in your office, telling you that the time had come. A time, that is, when it would look as if you were the target for the bomb. You were to get out to some spot near to the opening of Stillmore Lane where you could leave your car out of sight—I suppose there's some wood or some track there where it would be hidden in the darkness—get up the lane as fast as you could, dump the bomb and get back to your car. Then you were just to wait till everything was over. And the reason I've called this a notably cold-blooded crime is that you must have had that bomb ready to use in just the way you did for at least some weeks. You can't manufacture a bomb in a few minutes. And the reason you stayed here with your parents wasn't to be near Gwen. She never meant anything to you, though you managed to make your mother believe that she did as a smoke-screen for the real affair with Erica. The reason you stayed was just to be able to do what you did to Dearden when the chance came along."

"And is that all?" Jonathan asked.

"Of course not. There's the murder of Gwen to be explained. That wasn't as calculated as Dearden's murder, in fact it wasn't calculated at all. It was what happened because

things had gone wrong. She knew about you and Erica. I
don't know how she knew, but Gwen will have been the one
person who knew that there was nothing between her and
you, and that your attempt to make it look as if you were the
intended victim was absurd. But you saw a good deal of each
other and she may have known you far better than you realised. Something you said or did accidentally may have given
her the clue, and when Dearden died she must have worked
out how it had happened. She went up to London to visit
Erica and somehow got some admission out of her that was
very damaging to you. Yet she didn't go straight to the police
with her knowledge. She drove home, went to The Running
Man and rang you up, asking you to meet her there. And
when you did that, what she said to you had nothing to do
with her and Erica having believed that Nicholas was the
murderer, as you told me, and that you should go away because you were still in danger from him. She did tell you that
you were in danger and did beg you to go away, but that was
because, although she was going to give you the possibility of
escaping, she meant to go to the police next day. She didn't
want Nicholas suspected and she had enough feeling for you,
as someone whom she'd thought of as a friend, to want to
give you a chance. She even offered you money, didn't she, to
help you get out of the country from Heathrow?"

"So now we've got to Heathrow," Jonathan said. There
was irony in his voice. "I suppose you're going to explain
what in hell I was doing there, as apparently I wasn't expecting Gwen to join me."

"I think it was the best you could think of by way of setting up an alibi," Andrew said. "Not exactly an alibi, but it
publicised this supposed affair of yours with Gwen. It's unlikely that anyone noticed exactly when you got to the airport, in all the crowds there, and the forensic people can't say
to the minute when she died. And it only takes about an hour
to get from here to Heathrow—less, perhaps, in the middle of
the night when there's no traffic—so if you left as soon as

you'd dumped her body in the shed it would be hard for anyone to prove you hadn't been there at the time when she was killed."

"Hard to prove!" Jonathan exclaimed. "That's the first time anything about proof has been mentioned in all this. Do you really think anyone's going to believe you?"

"It wouldn't surprise me if Roland does," Andrew said. "It wouldn't surprise me if he and his men have already found the tracks of your car wherever you parked it beyond the end of the lane, and are getting ready to question you about them. If not, they'll do it when I've talked to them."

"And why did Gwen come out to talk to me in the middle of the night?" Jonathan asked. "You aren't suggesting I got inside the house to strangle her, are you?"

"She came out to give you some money, as she'd promised," Andrew said. "When she met you in The Running Man and tried to persuade you to go away, she offered you money to help you go, as I said just now. And you'd an appointment to meet her late in the night in the lane, where you'd be waiting for her, and she brought money down to you in her handbag, but instead of taking it you killed her and put her body in the shed. It always seemed a little strange to me, you know, that if you and she were going away together she shouldn't have gone with you in your car. What would have been the point of your driving off separately? But you made a real mistake, I'm afraid, picking up the handbag she dropped and putting it beside her in the shed. It would have been cleverer of you either to leave it where it had fallen, after taking the money out of it, so that it just could have looked as if she'd been assaulted and robbed after she came out of the house; or you could have taken it with you and thrown it into a ditch somewhere. It's interesting that you didn't think of helping yourself to the money. You aren't a thief. To each his particular form of crime. You're capable of murder, but it's against all your instincts to help yourself to someone else's money."

There was a short silence, then Jonathan suddenly sprang up from his chair and shot out of the room, slamming the door behind him. Andrew heard the sound of a key turning in the lock. So he was locked in.

It was really a great relief. It meant that there was nothing he could do for the present but sit still and finish his breakfast. He poured out a second cup of coffee for himself. He had not yet come to any decision as to what he would say to Colin and Dorothea, but beginning to think about this, and of how painful it was sure to be, he let his mind drift into memories. He thought of a holiday that he and Nell had once spent with the Cahills by the sea. Jonathan had been a child of ten, with bright eyes and a glowing smile and the wonderful charm of childish exuberance together with apparently warm affections. He and Andrew had played French cricket together on the beach, and as often as he had been able, Jonathan would hook the old tennis ball with which they were playing into the waves, so that Andrew had to go wading into the surf to recover it while Jonathan crowed with laughter. Andrew had enjoyed the game quite as much as the boy. And Jonathan had had an enormous appetite, zestfully gorging on huge helpings of roast beef and Yorkshire pudding, on cream teas and strawberries, and on anything else attractive that came near him. Then he would fling his arms round his mother and kiss her and tell her that it had been wonderful. Was there any of that child still left in him? Was that what had drawn Erica Haslam to him, his sheer enjoyment of good things and eagerness to obtain them at any price?

At that point Andrew deliberately directed his thoughts elsewhere. He did not want to start interpreting Jonathan's motives or actions. He began to think about Robert Hooke and the contract that he had signed for the publication of his book. He began to think about the next chapter that should be written, for which he had abundant notes. It would be the last chapter in the book and if he really settled down to work, should not take him more than two or three weeks to finish.

But what a loss it would be to him when the work was finally done. Until he brought himself to start on something else, his days would be empty. It was one of his misfortunes that he had no hobbies. He thought of a colleague of his who on his retirement had settled down with great pleasure to painting watercolours, usually of flowers, some of which he even sold occasionally. Something like that must make old age much easier to endure. But the fate of Robert Hooke was sealed. There was that contract: a challenge, if nothing else.

It was ten o'clock when the moment came that Andrew had been dreading. He heard the key turn in the lock, the door opened and Colin came in.

"So he locked you in," Colin said.

"Yes," Andrew answered.

"He's gone, you know." Colin's tone was flat and expressionless.

"Do you know where to?" Andrew asked.

"No."

"I don't suppose he does either."

"No, I don't suppose so."

"Has he told you . . . ?" Andrew hesitated as Colin stood still in the middle of the room, looking at him in a dull, tired way as if there was nothing for them to discuss.

"Yes, I think he told us most of it," he said.

"Colin, I'm sorry . . ."

"Nothing you could help. You're going to the police, of course."

"I've got to, haven't I?"

"I think so, yes."

"It's what you'd do yourself, is it?"

"That's a different question. I doubt if I could bring myself to do it. But of course it ought to be done. Not that Dorothea and I understand the whole of it. But when you're ready will you come down and tell us how you worked things out?"

"I'll come now, if that's what you want."

"All right, come along then."

Andrew stood up.

"Colin, I think I ought to go home today," he said. "I'm ready to go right away."

"I suppose that would be best. Only you'll have to go and talk to Roland first. Meanwhile . . ." This time it was Colin who hesitated.

"Yes?" Andrew said.

"They'll catch up with him, won't they, wherever he's gone? But at least he got away from here. He's got a chance. I believe you meant him to have it, talking to him so early up here."

Andrew thought that Jonathan had a chance to drive over the edge of a cliff, if that was what he preferred to being arrested and tried, but not much chance of any other escape.

"You know, he said to me there wasn't any proof of what I was saying to him," he said. "It may be that there isn't much proof that would stand up in a court of law."

"He's admitted it all to us, as I told you," Colin said, "and when pressure's put on her, I think Erica's liable to break down. She may try her best to put the whole blame for the plot on him, though it seems to me likely enough to have been her idea originally. But I know it's only natural that I should think like that. And perhaps I don't really. Whatever the truth is about that, we've got to recognize that Jonathan is a danger to himself and others. Come along, Andrew. Don't be afraid of meeting Dorothea. She's much stronger than you may imagine."

They went downstairs together. Dorothea and Lyn Goddard were together in the sitting-room. Andrew noticed as he went in that the holly that had been tucked in above the picture frames was gone, and so was the bough that had been hung with Christmas cards. He saw too that Dorothea's eyes were red and that her face was blotched and pale. She looked at him, but it was as if she were looking through him and did not see him. As usual she was on the sofa with her knees drawn up to her chin. Lyn was standing by a window, look-ing out, and did not turn when Colin and Andrew entered.

"Andrew's going home today," Colin said, with the same lifeless tone in which he had spoken upstairs. "But first he's got to see Roland. I'll drive him into Rockford presently."

Lyn turned quickly. "I'll do that. I'll take Nicholas's car. You two had better stay together."

"But I still only half understand things," Dorothea said. "Please explain it all to us, Andrew. Jonathan said you could."

"I can tell you what I said to him," Andrew said.

"Then do that, please."

"I don't know how much he told you."

"He said—only it didn't sound like him saying it, he sounded so wild—he said he's the murderer they're looking for and he did it because he was in love with Erica, and Erica hated her father and wanted his money, and Gwen found out about it and was going to go to the police. And he said some-thing about Erica making a telephone call to his office, which I don't understand, and that we'd never see him again."

"Then he gave you the substance of what I had to say," Andrew said.

"But please explain it."

Sitting down, Andrew began to repeat what he had said to Jonathan. None of them asked any questions. As he spoke, it occurred to Andrew that this was probably the last time that he would ever see Colin and Dorothea, unless it was in a court room, and he recognized that although for some years they had not seen a great deal of one another, their friendship had been deeply valued through much of his life. If he could have thought of any way of sparing them, he would have done so. But they did not seem to want it. All that they wanted just then was certainty, to know exactly what it was that they would have to face.

Colin had sat down on the sofa, and he and Dorothea moved closer to one another while Andrew spoke, Colin putting an arm round Dorothea and she resting her head against his shoulder. Lyn stayed by the window to which she had turned once more, gazing out into the garden.

When Andrew had come to the end of what he had to say there was silence in the room.

Then Dorothea raised her head and said, "Of course I always knew it."

"Knew that Jonathan was . . ." Andrew began in astonishment, then stopped himself.

"Was the murderer?" she said. "No, of course not, I didn't know that. But I knew he was very unhappy about something, and he wouldn't talk to me as he used to. I thought it was because of Gwen. He's been a different boy for some time now, and I used to think he'd be better off if he didn't live here with us and see her so often. But you say that had nothing to do with it. If he gets life now for what he's done, he'll be an old man when he comes out and we'll both be dead."

Colin's hold of her tightened and she let her head rest on his shoulder again.

"We'll move away," he said. "Go to London or somewhere anonymous. But we'll have to stay here for the present, I suppose. We must get a lawyer and see what can be done. Everything you told us is circumstantial, isn't it, Andrew? There's just the question of tyre tracks in the wood down the lane and the telephone call Erica made to the office, if the hospital has a record of it. And that he ever made any confession to us is something we don't have to tell anyone. But then again, perhaps . . ." He paused. "When you've committed two murders, does it get easier to commit another, several others? I suppose it does."

Andrew did not feel that he had to answer. That for every murderer there were parents, or a husband or a wife, or children, or friends who might suffer almost as much as his victims—this was something he had always known but to which he had never given any special thought. In a general way he had always assumed that they were to be blamed if they gave any succour to the man of violence. But looking two people in the face, two people who now had the horror of choice of action thrust upon them, was very confusing.

He drew a deep breath and said, "Well, I'd better be going."

Lynn turned again. "To the police?"

"Yes."

"I'll take you."

"Thank you."

He went upstairs to fetch the suitcase that he had packed. When he came down again Colin and Dorothea were still sitting side by side on the sofa with their backs to the door. They did not look round as he came to it, and he did not go into the room. Lyn was waiting for him in the hall, putting on her overcoat. Andrew went to the front door without speaking.

He and Lyn did not talk as they walked together to the Deardens' garage. She backed Nicholas's car out and Andrew got in beside her. She drove very slowly along the narrow lane, but as they reached the end of it and emerged onto the main road she suddenly accelerated, driving far faster than was advisable along a road with so many bends and ups and downs. Andrew hated to be driven fast, but glancing sideways at her set face, he managed to say nothing. He felt that she almost wanted to be involved in an accident, or at least to put as much distance as she could between herself and Upper Cullonden, as rapidly as was possible.

After a little while she slowed down somewhat and said, "You know, I thought it was Henry."

"It was Henry you meant in the pub, was it, when you said you knew who it was?" Andrew asked.

"Yes, but not for any good reason," she said. "It was just a feeling I had about him. I don't usually trust my feelings so rashly. I don't think I'll do it again."

"You didn't know about Jonathan and Erica?"

"No."

"But now Henry will have to know."

"Yes, poor Henry. But it doesn't really break my heart. I don't think it can ever have been much of a marriage."

"Are you going to trust your feelings about Nicholas?"

"If he wants me to."

"Have you any doubts about that?"

"I always have doubts about everything. If I could be sure that it'll be the same for us as it is for Colin and Dorothea—though why they should have had a son like Jonathan . . . It can't have been their fault. The Jonathans of this world seem just to happen without anyone being specially to blame. Perhaps it's genetic. You never had any children yourself, did you?"

"No."

"Were you sorry?"

"Well, I said to myself, we live in an overcrowded world, so why worry?"

"That was sensible. I don't think I want any children. Too much of a risk."

"You know, I've a feeling that in a few years you'll have two or three at least crawling around you. One has to take risks sometimes."

She did not answer for some time, then at last, thoughtfully, said, "Yes."

They hardly spoke again until she drove him up to the entrance of the police station in Rockford.

Andrew spent about the next two hours talking to Detective Inspector Roland and Sergeant Porter. They agreed that for once the weathermen had been right, that a frost had come as they had predicted, and that this might be the beginning of a severe winter. On the other hand, it might not. There might be a mild breeze, perhaps a little rain and a sodden sense of mildness by tomorrow. After that matter had been settled, their talk became more demanding.

Sergeant Porter took copious notes. Roland took Andrew

over his statement again and again, by degrees making him feel as time went on how thin his story was and by how few facts it was supported. Yet he was told that tyre tracks had been found in the wood at the end of Stillmore Lane, and though it was thought that these might have been left by a courting couple who had found it a convenient place to park out of sight from the main road, there was also a suspicion that the tracks might match with the tyres of Jonathan's car. But Jonathan and his car had vanished for the moment.

Some days later Andrew heard that Jonathan's car had been found in the car-park at Heathrow, but whether Jonathan had really left the country for some destination not yet discovered, or had simply left his car at the airport as a blind while he stayed in hiding in Britain, was not known. However, the tyres of the car matched the tracks that had been left in the wood.

The matter of the telephone call to Jonathan's office was simpler. While Andrew and Roland were talking in Rockford, Sergeant Porter had at one point left the room, and returning after a while had nodded his head at the inspector. It appeared that he had been able to check that Erica Haslam had made a telephone call to Rockford not long after she had been admitted to the hospital. Challenged later, she coolly admitted it. Henry Haslam was frantic, and denied that it was possible and immediately engaged lawyers to defend his wife. As long as he possibly could, he refused to believe that she could be in love with anyone but himself. When she quietly killed herself by taking an overdose of barbiturates one day after emerging from St. Raphael's, he mourned her as a beloved wife who had never recovered from the after-effects of her accident.

Jonathan Cahill vanished into thin air. A man's body that was found in the Thames many weeks after the murders and never identified was thought possibly to be his, but this was never certain. It was not impossible that he was making a good career for himself, might have married, had children and even settled down in Chile or Peru or some other country. Thinking of Colin and Dorothea, Andrew favoured this belief, though he had no evidence for doing so.

After his long session in the police station in Rockford, at the end of which he had signed a statement, a police car had driven him to the station and he had returned home. He had never before felt that he loved his home so much. For a long time after Nell's death its emptiness had had almost a feeling of menace for him. He had thought of moving to a smaller flat, or even into the country. But then there would have been the appalling problem to be faced of what to do with all his books; and of deciding which pieces of furniture, collected by Nell and him over the years, he could bear to part with; and of finding someone as comfortably efficient as his daily help to keep things in order. In the end he had stayed where he was, the number of books relentlessly increasing, so that he had had to have new book-shelves built for him. His help had left him, but he had been fortunate in soon finding another. And the presence of Nell never altogether faded from rooms that slowly became shabbier, yet were dear to his heart. He often talked to Nell when he was there alone, finding it easy to fill in the replies that she never made. Arriving home after the most distressing Christmas of his experience, he told her bit by bit all that had happened to him during the last few days.

But at the same time he began to think of Robert Hooke and of his contract. A contract was a serious thing. He sat down at his desk and began to turn over some of the pages of notes lying there. If he really worked at it he could finish the book quite soon. He slid a sheet of paper into his typewriter.

About the Author

E. X. Ferrars, who lives in England, is the author of over sixty works of mystery and suspense, including *Trial by Fury* and *Woman Slaughter*. She has received a special award by the British Crime Writers Association for continuing excellence in the mystery field.